MW01154414

THE MYSTERY OF THE FIVE ORANGES

A NEW SHERLOCK HOLMES MYSTERY

CRAIG STEPHEN COPLAND

With the original Sherlock Holmes story,
The Five Orange Pips,
included

Copyright © 2014 by Craig Stephen Copland

All rights reserved. No part of this book that has been written by Craig Stephen Copland may be reproduced or transmitted in any form or by any means, electronic or mechanical, including photocopying, recording, or by an information storage and retrieval system – except by a reviewer who may quote brief passages in a review to be printed in a magazine, newspaper, or on the web – without permission in writing from Craig Stephen Copland.

The characters of Sherlock Holmes and Dr. Watson are in the public domain, as is the original story, *The Five Orange Pips*.

Anne of Green Gables, by Lucy Maud Montgomery, is in the public domain, as are the characters in the book.

Published by:

Conservative Growth
1101 30th Street NW. Ste. 500
Washington, DC 20007

Cover design by Rita Toews.

ISBN: 1502788756

ISBN-13:   978-1502788757

DEDICATION

To my three daughters – Lydia, Esther and Charis – who read and fell in love with *Anne of Green Gables* twenty-five years before I finally did.

CONTENTS

ACKNOWLEDGMENTS

This novella borrows extensively from the sacred canon of Sherlock Holmes stories by Arthur Conan Doyle, and from *Anne of Green Gables*, by Lucy Maud Montgomery. Both of these writers and their stories are among the finest in literature. They have never been out of print and continue to sell in the millions. I am indebted to both of them not just for the use made of their stories but for the continuing joy they give me as I read them over and over again.

The plot of this novella is inspired by the Sherlock Holmes story, *The Five Orange Pips*. Your enjoyment of this book will be enhanced by a quick re-read of that short but intriguing story. It is appended to this novella and should be read first if you never have or cannot remember it.

My dearest and best friend, Mary Engelking, read all drafts, helped with whatever historical and geographical accuracy was required, and offered insightful recommendations for changes to the narrative structure, characters, and dialogue. Thank you.

The Downtown Oakville Writers' Group has endured drafts of all of my Sherlock Holmes stories and made innumerable useful recommendations for improvement. Thank you.

Many words and whole phrases and sentences have been lifted and copied shamelessly and joyfully from the sacred canon of Sherlockian literature. Should any word or turn of phrase strike the reader as the *mot juste*, you may count on its having been plagiarized.

1 THE STORMY VISITOR

When I look back through my notes of the many cases that came across the threshold of 221B Baker Street I have to pause at the year of 1908. It was a remarkable year in many ways. We see it now as the pinnacle of the Edwardian Era, the most golden year of the Golden Age. A third of all of the inhabitants of the earth were citizens of the British Empire and except for a few minor skirmishes the world was at peace and we all believed, oh so wrongly, that peace, progress and prosperity would continue unabated for decades to come.

Yet the signs were there, if only we all, like Sherlock Holmes, could have not just looked but truly observed. Had the Foreign Office heeded the warning of England's finest detective, the King of Portugal would not have been assassinated, nor an attempt made on the life of the Shah of Iran. Fortunately after that nasty incident in Persia the British government moved quickly to secure for the Empire the rights to all Persian oil, thereby assuring long-term future stability in the Levant. Our gracious sovereign, Edward VII, had personally intervened and smoothed over relations between England,

France, and Russia but had made little progress with his obstreperous cousin, Kaiser Wilhelm II, who insisted on trying to build more Dreadnoughts than sailed under the Union Jack – a sign that some rough times with the Germans lay ahead.

Holmes also had to intervene or the glorious Olympic Games, hastily relocated to London after an inconsiderate eruption of Mount Vesuvius made them unaffordable for Italy, would have ended in an ignominious quagmire of cheating, fixed scores and bribed judges. He received no public credit for his service and again spurned the offer of a knighthood from those he deemed imbecilic enough to have needed his services.

1908 was also the year when, in private, the English had to admit that we were being surpassed constantly by the Americans on all fronts. They had not only invented manned flight but the world's first pilot, Orrville Wright, wondrously flew an airplane for over one hour without landing. Their intrepid explorer, not ours, Robert Perry, was the first man to set foot on the North Pole. Their industrialist, not ours, Henry Ford, began producing automobiles on his assembly line and selling them to the public at prices that could not be imagined in England or on the Continent. Even that bedrock of the Empire, the British Fleet, had been outclassed by the Great White Fleet of sixteen massive battleships and numerous supporting vessels that President Roosevelt had sent, to delirious awe, to the ports of call in the circumnavigated globe.

We did not know it then, but it was one of the last great years of an era that would soon be destroyed and never to be seen again.

It was also the year of one of the most unusual cases presented to Sherlock Holmes. While on the surface it was reported as merely the solving of a string of everyday murders, behind it was the emasculating and dismantling of one of the most dastardly criminal organizations ever to have wrought evil upon the various human races. It demanded not only the application of his great analytical skill but also, from Sherlock Holmes as well as from an unusual group of brave citizens, profound physical courage in the presence of grave danger. It is this case, the one I have called *The Mystery of the Five Oranges,* that I now share with our loyal readers.

It began with a complete absence of pomp and circumstance; the opposite in fact. It was the most miserable of many miserable rainy days in London. The equinoctial gales of late September brought in sheets of rain that swept up and down Baker Street, vanishing pedestrians and all but the most desperate of cabbies. The storm had continued unabated into the eighth hour of the evening when only the vague glow from the gas lamps on the pavement below could be seen from our bay window. In response to an unexpected clatter of a carriage I glanced out and discerned a cab stopping in front of our door. A man descended and attempted to open an umbrella, only to have it turned inside out by a gust of wind. I watched as the poor wet soul paid the driver and then turned and knocked on our door. Mrs. Hudson, always the most considerate of English women, scurried to the door so as not to leave anyone standing out in the elements.

"Are you expecting a client, Holmes?" I asked. "At this hour?"

"I had not been," Holmes replied, with a faint smile appearing on his face. "Yet now I am expecting that whoever is about to come through our door is quite likely to become my client and a rather interesting one. No common boring case would be arriving at a time and on a day like this. So, yes, my good doctor, I am now eagerly expecting our next client."

"Mr. John Openshaw," announced Mrs. Hudson, as she opened the door and ushered in a rather wet tall, gaunt man in his forties. "Let me take you coat, sir, and you sit right here and dry off by the fire," she said in her predictable concerned manner. "I'll get you a hot cup of tea."

She pulled out a spare chair and turned it so that its back was to the fire and hung the man's fine wool coat over it. He sat in the settee opposite Sherlock Holmes, pushed off his shoes and stretched his wet stockinged feet towards the hearth.

"You should have come here over six months ago," said Sherlock Holmes, "when whatever it is that is distressing you first took place. Dr. Watson and I conduct our affairs in complete confidence and your seeking my assistance would have remained a secret outside of these walls, a matter that no doubt concerns you greatly."

The newest client of Sherlock Holmes looked at him with that same look of shock and wonder that I have seen on countless clients as Holmes revealed to them that he already knew more about them than they would have ever thought possible. Mrs. Hudson appeared with a tray of hot tea that she set in front of our visitor. Observing the stupefied look on his face she gave a bit of a sideways look to Sherlock Holmes and gave a pat on the hand to our visitor. "There, there, sir. Don't let him intimidate you. Just tell him your story. He really is quite good at helping."

For a moment Mr. Openshaw just stared first at Mrs. Hudson and then at Holmes. Then he spoke. "It was nine months ago. You are right, although I cannot for the life of me know how you knew that. And yes, it must remain a secret. I am being watched and followed constantly. I have been warned that if I go to Scotland Yard they will kill her. If they knew that I had come to see you they would kill her." With these words he lost control and dropped his head into his hands and remained that way for some time. I noted, as did Holmes, that he spoke with an American accent, one that had a trace of a southern drawl.

When he raised his head Holmes replied to him. "Who are 'they' and who would they kill?"

"She is my daughter. No. In truth she is not legally my daughter but I have been her guardian for the past five years and have raised her and loved her like a daughter and she has loved me as her father. She is now just fifteen years old. They kidnapped her nine months ago. They will kill her if I reveal anything about them or go to the police. I am at my wits end, Mr. Holmes. I am here in desperation. I fear that something has happened to her. She…"

"Who are 'they,' said Holmes brusquely, interrupting him.

Our newest client gripped the arms of the chair very tightly and fought to regain his composure. "They are the most vile, evil organization on the face of the earth. They are not operating here in Britain but they have spies everywhere. They are active all over America but by far are strongest in the southern states. They are insanely committed to the belief that North America belongs only to those who are white, gentile and Protestant. They alone are the masters. All other races and religions must be kept in subservience to them. They are prepared to steal, burn, rape, pillage and murder those they believe to be in opposition to their hateful vision. They may appear comical, costumed in bed sheets and dunce hats, but when they ride en masse into a neighborhood and plant a burning cross on the lawn of one of their enemies they strike terror into the hearts of all. They call themselves the Ku Klux Klan."

"I know of this organization," said Holmes. "It was formed by some veterans of the Confederate States following the loss of their war. It was my understanding that they had succeeded in their quest to remove the vote from the negro and Republicans from office, and install Democrat segregationists throughout the southern United States. Having done that, they disbanded and ceased to be an active organized political force. Are you telling me that they remain active and have threatened your life and your daughter's? But pray, let us not get ahead of ourselves. Give us the essential facts of your case from the commencement, and I can afterwards question you as to those details which seem to me to be most important."

"Very well, sir," Mr. Openshaw replied. He paused and then began his story. "My father, Joseph Openshaw, was born in Coventry, not far from the great cathedral and to very pious parents. But he had an adventurous soul and when he turned eighteen he elected to give himself over to his animal spirits, left home, and emigrated to America. He had heard that there were grants of land being given to settlers in Florida and so he went there and settled in the city of St. Augustine. That would have been the year of 1860. The War Between the States broke out soon after he had set foot in the new world. Florida succeeded from the Union in January of 1861 and he was immediately recruited, under some duress, to join the Confederate Army. He never spoke of his years during the war. I gathered that he went through hell and back again and was grateful to have come out alive with all of his wits and all of his limbs. So many others did not. He also emerged with a tight group of comrades, a band of brothers, who had shared the horrors of that war, stuck by each other, and saved each other's lives countless times. They were bound together by hoops of steel, as they say, and would die before letting harm ever come to any one of them. Or so my father believed.

"He returned to Florida and convinced his Confederate brothers to do so as well. Most of them went into some sort of agricultural endeavor such as cattle, or sheep, or citrus trees, or sugar, but my father, having had a proper English schooling, was not for farming. He acquired a tract of land in a small port called Boca Raton. The name is Spanish and sounds quite exotic and all, unless of course one happens to know the Spanish tongue and then you know that it means "mouth of the rat" which is not very exotic or even attractive. Nevertheless that was where he lived and he set up his small factory. He was very handy and he saw a need for a new type of boat that could traverse the great dismal swamps they called The Everglades. So he put a bicycle on top of a flat-bottomed skiff and removed the back wheel and with a few gears and belts connected it to a big propeller that sat on top of the boat, spun like that of an airplane, and sped the boat over the top of the waters of the glades. He called his craft the Openshaw Bicycle Boat. They sold well and he made a small fortune off of them. He made some larger ones that he outfitted with a small steam engine. They were very popular with everybody except for the waterfowl who did not get along well with open propellers. No sooner had that new cereal, shredded wheat, been introduced at the World's Fair in Chicago in 1893 that some wag started calling my father's boat 'Shredded Tweet Boats' which was very droll, but I digress."

"Very droll, indeed. No doubt appealing to the American sense of humor," said Holmes. "Pray continue with the facts of your case."

"In 1870," he continued, "my father met my mother, Rachel Adams, a fine young southern woman from a family in Palm Beach, and they were married a year later. I was born in late 1871 but tragically my mother did not survive childbirth. I was raised by maids and governesses in what, for south Florida of that day, was as close to a genteel upbringing as could be hoped for.

"It was also in the early 1870s that some of my father's Confederate brothers became associated with the organization now known as the Ku Klux Klan. At first it was presented to my father as similar in intent to the Rochdale movement, and formed so that southern merchants and landowners could cooperate together, combine their strength and actions and fight off the unscrupulous Yankee carpetbaggers who were stealing our land, our businesses, our houses, and our way of life. Father was quite sympathetic to the Rochdale ideals and had known some members of the local cooperatives in Coventry and Birmingham, and as he had complete trust in his band of brothers he joined them. Many of the southern men had little or no schooling and as my father had received a good grammar school education in England and was skilled in writing and numbers, at least by comparison to his fellows, they made him the Secretary of the organization for their local band. Within a year he had been promoted to Secretary of the Klan for the State. By 1880 he was Secretary for the entire national organization. He was a diligent and organized man and kept all the files and minutes and membership roles in good order and made sure that they were preserved and protected, as any good Secretary is supposed to do.

"It is hard for me to understand how my father, who was not a man of violence or hatred, could have served such a vile organization. He was an Englishman, of course, and so considered that all other nations and races were inferior. The negro was not his equal, but then neither was the Frenchman nor the Dutchman. And the negro was clearly a good notch above the average Spaniard or Greek. But he had no desire to do harm to anyone. It was just that all men of his age and place joined the Klan at that time. Only a very few of them of them practiced the doing of violence to negro freemen, Jews, Catholics and Republicans. The rest simply belonged and took no action to stop the evil. Laws were passed eventually and the Klan was suppressed, but it never died. Nor did my father ever destroy all the member rolls and records that had been entrusted to him as the national secretary. He kept them safely stored away under lock and key in a bank in Miami.

"As a boy growing up in my father's home I heard very little about the early activities of the Klan. Father's business continued to prosper and he made astute investments in various enterprises. He was a minor partner with Henry Flagler and invested in the railways that linked the coast of Florida with the rest of America, and in the magnificent Breakers Hotel in Palm Beach, which for the past decade has been the most luxurious abode south of Savannah. He became a wealthy man. Our life was very good indeed, sir."

"Until?" said Holmes, with a touch of impatience in his voice.

"Until eight years ago, when I was married."

"Did you marry against your father's wishes," asked Holmes.

"No not against Father's. But against the wishes of all of his old Confederate brothers, and against the strict rules of the Klan. You see, sir, my wife was a negro."

"That would cause some consternation for the Ku Klux Klan," observed Holmes.

"My wife was an exceptionally beautiful, talented and gracious Christian woman, sir. Her father was the pastor of the African Baptist Church. Her mother was the organist and a gifted musician. My wife graduated from Bennett College and served as a teacher in our local high school. She was respected by all of the families and I counted myself blessed beyond imagining that she took an interest in me and when she agreed to be my bride and the mother of my children I thought I would die with happiness.

"The families of our village and of Palm Beach were quite encouraging of our union. I was well-known because of my father's success and some thought me to be a very eligible bachelor, and, as I said, my wife was the belle of Boca Raton. It never occurred to me that years after the activities of the Klan had faded away that there would still be old members who held such strong views on the miscegenation of the races that they would seek to destroy our lives.

"Our first warning came when my betrothal was announced. Father received a note in the mail from two of his old Confederate brothers respectfully explaining that my impending marriage was contrary to the laws of Nature and God and should be called off. Father sent a letter back to them and said that while he continued to value their friendship he would have to disagree as he placed no value on any argument against the mixing of the races.

"Another warning was received on the eve of our wedding. This one was much harsher and included a threat that our family would have to face consequences. Now my father had not risen to his level of success by being a timorous man. He did not take well to being threatened and he sent a harsh reply back to his former friends. But being a cautious man he also hired two large young colored men to serve as night watchmen at our home. One of them was later killed, his death attributed to unknown circumstances and by persons unknown.

"My wife and I were treated with respect in our community regardless of our racial difference, although that may have been the result less of the enlightened beliefs of our neighbors than our being one of the wealthiest families in the town. Actions taken by the rich are always excusable in a way they might not be for the poor.

"My dear wife and I wished to have a family but discovered that after two years of failing to conceive a child that she was barren. We elected then to adopt children and raise them as our own and we let our intentions be known to our friends and family. The rumor spread however that my wife was in the family way and we were expecting a child. Our friends congratulated us and even when given the facts of the matter continued to give us their best wishes. But then we received anonymous messages, signed only with the letters "K.K.K.". We were shocked by the antipathy of so many people to the breeding of children of mixed race. Some contained the most vile language and terrible threats against us. My father counseled that only cowards would refuse to sign their names and that we should have no concern about them. To this day I pray to God that he had not been so naïve.

"In September of the year 1902, six years ago, after completing all the arrangements required, I journeyed north to Savannah. There is an orphanage there and they were caring for many children, including some of Irish parentage, and I was awarded the most blessed gift of a beautiful little girl of nine years of age. It was a moment of great joy and I could not wait to return to my wife and share such a blessing with her. I brought her back with me to Palm Beach County only to have my joy turn to ashes. I arrived to find that the night before my home had burned to the ground and my wife and father had died in the inferno. It was only by fate, or Providence, that I happened to be away and thus was spared. The sheriff determined that it was a tragic accident likely caused by a faulty gaslight but on the charred remnants of my front door were scratched the letters "K K K" and I knew that it was the work of the Klan.

"While my spirit seethed with a desire for revenge I knew in my heart that I now had the responsibility as a father of a young daughter and that I had to govern myself with prudence. I knew I could not live in peace any longer in the southern states and so I liquidated all my family's assets and interests. My father, and consequently I, still had title to a small estate near Coventry and so I came to England and have attempted to build a life for my daughter and me here. As a measure to insure our safety, or so I thought, I also transferred to Lloyds Bank all the old records and files of the Klan that my father had faithfully preserved from decades earlier. In those files were the names of all of the members of the Klan in years past, and a record of many of the crimes they had committed. Through intermediaries I let it be known that if any harm were ever to come to me, my solicitors had instructions to release all of these records to Scotland Yard and thence to the American Department of Justice in Washington. It would mean exposure and imprisonment for many of the senior members of the Klan who had secretly preserved its web of Klansmen, and were taking steps to re-establish it as a force of political terror throughout the North American continent.

"With that safeguard in place I lived an open life with my daughter in our new home near Coventry. I purchased and improved a small factory producing bicycle tires, and have expanded our production to include tires for automobiles, which are to be the method of transport of the twentieth century. We, my daughter and I, had a very good life for the past five years but then just before Christmas all that was snatched away from me. I returned to my house after doing some shopping in the Coventry High Street only to find that my servants had been beaten senseless and tied up, and that my daughter had vanished. On my dining room table was a letter addressed to me. Here it is."

Our client reached into his suitcoat pocket and produced an envelope that he handed to Holmes. He read it and handed it to me. It ran:

> As you have chosen to use our records as your insurance policy, so we will use your daughter as ours.
>
> You will keep and guard our records safely and secretly in England.
>
> Should any of them become known to the public or given to the police,
>
> Should you make contact with the police either in England or in the United States of America, or
>
> Should you in any way attempt to come to America to retrieve your daughter, be advised:
>
> She will be violated, crucified and burned at the stake.
>
> We have agents everywhere. You are being watched.
>
> Govern yourself accordingly.
>
> **K K K**

"Good heavens!" I exclaimed. "What sort of depraved vicious monsters would even make such a threat?"

"They would not just make it," said Mr. Openshaw. "They would make good on it. Their minds are so twisted and their methods so terrifying that I have no doubt they would do exactly what they are threatening.

"You may understand, sir," he said, returning to face Holmes, "that my life for the past nine months has been a sheer hell. I have made discreet inquiries through a few trusted friends. One of them is known to you; Major Pendergast. He said that you helped him in the past and that I must come and seek your involvement. Sir, I beseech you. I have done everything I can think of. I have hardly slept or eaten for months."

"Pardon me, sir," interrupted Holmes. "Please hold your story there for just a moment and permit me to ask one or two questions."

The man nodded. Instead of asking his questions Holmes closed his eyes and for a full two minutes looked as if he had entered a trance. He body and head were stationery but his lips were moving ever so little. Mr. Openshaw gazed at him in bewilderment and then looked over at me. I held up my hand indicating that he should be patient as I watched Sherlock Holmes mentally reviewing the hundreds of documents that were stored in his memory and now being re-read again in that photographic mind of his. Then his body indicated a small start, his eyes popped open and his head lifted.

"Aha. Yes. Permit me to ask you sir. Is the name of your daughter perchance Belinda?"

"Why yes," said the surprised client. "I had not stated her name, had I? How did you know that?"

"You said that her biological lineage was Irish, but is her appearance and complexion exceptional even for an Irish lass? Is her hair unusually red in color and her skin freckled?"

"Yes, but how did you know that?"

"And is she what you might call precocious; highly articulate for a child of her age, and given to unusual flights of imagination and creativity?"

"Yes. Yes. That is her. That is exactly what she is like. But how could you have possibly known that?"

"I have had some intelligence about your situation from a source that I had not considered to be reliable, but your story has now confirmed what I was told. But do tell me, sir, why now? Why have you chosen to seek my help after nine months of not having done so?"

Our client continued to look at Holmes with intense curiosity and spoke slowly. "Her captors permit her to send a letter to me every two months to prove that she is still alive. Her messages are strictly censored so as not to give any clues as to her whereabouts and are sent to me through a mailing service office in New York City. I have tried to penetrate that office only to find that the owners are in league with the Klan. I received letters in February, April, and June, all simply saying that she was well, that she loved me, and that she was doing her best to keep up her studies. They were written in her hand and I knew that she was still in good health. Yesterday, however, I received a letter from her, posted at the end of August that was in her hand but the contents were very unlike what I had received previously. I believe that she is now enduring some sort of torture and suffering and I am now completely desperate. So I took the risk of coming to you in the midst of an evening storm hoping that there was no chance of my being followed."

"Do you have her letters?" asked Holmes.

Mr. Openshaw handed several envelopes to Holmes. He read each of them and in turn passed them on to me. The first three were as the girl's father had described them. The fourth was indeed unlike the others. It ran:

> Dearest Father:
>
> I am well. Are you well? Missing you I am. Is it sunny in England? Now that it is summer. Can you enjoy your garden? Are you watering your flowers? Not that you do not in the spring. Any flower needs water. Do you not agree? Always they do.
>
> Your loving daughter,
>
> Bel

"Do you see what I mean?" the distressed father said. "This is so unlike her. Something terrible must have happened. Is there anything you can do? What have you heard about her? What?"

A faint smile flickered at the corners of Holmes's mouth. "You daughter is not in any greater danger than before, and she is bravely taking matters into her own hands."

"Sir, what are you saying?" said Mr. Openshaw. I had to admit that I too was puzzled.

"Mr. Openshaw, Doctor Watson, please just read the true message of this letter by observing only the first letter of each sentence this ingenious young woman has written"

The father and I looked again at the note.

I A M I N C A N A D A

"In Canada?" I exclaimed. "That is very strange indeed. What could the Ku Klux Klan possibly be doing in Canada?"

"That," said Holmes, "we do not know. But clearly she is there and has let us know."

"I would go there straightaway," said Mr. Openshaw. "But I am being watched and they would know about it immediately. Could you, Mr. Holmes? Is there any possible way? I assure you that expense is no object? I know it is a great deal to ask of you. But . . ."

"I believe that I could put aside some other matters and make a brief journey across the pond," said Holmes. "And my good doctor, is there any possibility you could do likewise?"

I acknowledged that I could. My dear wife was visiting her family in the west and my list of patients was not pressing.

"Before you leave, sir," said Holmes to Mr. Openshaw. "You said that all of the records of the Klan were safely stored at Lloyds Bank, did you not? You do have the key and the number of the secured locker where they are kept?"

"Yes. But I cannot touch them. It would become known immediately and my Belinda would be in danger. Lloyds has assured me that no one other than I can ever be given access. It is impossible for anyone else to view them without my written authorization, and that would also become known."

Again the same faint smile appeared on Holmes face. "Mr. Openshaw," he said. "If I am to take on this case you will have to trust me with your life and with that of your daughter. I assure you that no harm will come to either of you that is in any way touching upon the records stored at Lloyds. May I have the key and the number of your secured locker, sir?"

Hesitantly the client handed over a small envelope to Holmes who in turn handed it to me with a knowing nod. Inaudibly I mouthed back one word to him. "Mycroft?" He again nodded.

"Sir," Holmes said rising to his feet, "you and your precious daughter are good people who have been caught in the web of those who are evil. This KKK organization is clearly active, organized, determined and dangerous. I had not suspected that their tentacles extended all the way to Canada and even to England. But clearly they do, and I assure you sir that I will do my utmost to secure the safe return of your daughter, and to diminish or even destroy those who are threatening you. I shall forward telegrams and letters through Major Pendergast and you should do likewise. Now sir, I bid you good evening and please do take care of yourself for your daughter's sake."

Holmes took our client's coat, now warm and dry, from the back of the chair on which it had rested and handed it to him. He nodded and shook our hands and departed back into the dark and stormy night.

2 THE PRECOCIOUS LETTER

As soon as the door had closed I turned to Holmes.

"Very well Holmes, even I could tell that he desired to be secretive about his visit, else he would not have come at so late an hour an in such inclement weather. But how did you know that the kidnapping had happened months ago. And from where, in heaven's name, did you uncover the name of his daughter?"

"His clothes were expensive and finely tailored," said Holmes. "Yet they hung on him as if they had been supplied by Omar the Tent Maker. He has clearly lost at least three stone since his clothes were measured, something that no one can do in short order. He has been in deep distress for months. As to his daughter's name, I have you to thank for that." As he spoke he walked to a set of square metal canisters that were stacked behind the settee and in which he kept his files of correspondence.

"Me? That is silly, Holmes. I have no idea whatsoever about the matters of this case and certainly none about the man's poor daughter."

"Ah," he replied. "But through your ridiculously romanticized stories in *The Strand* you have made my name common in households throughout the world, and because of you I receive no end of letters from adoring fans, terribly amateur detectives, and suspicious people suspecting crimes and conspiracies. Most are imbecilic nonsense. Just in today's post was one asking for help finding the criminals who were responsible for raising taxes on brandy. I sent a note back saying that although such taxes were undeniably criminal they were, sadly, totally legal." As he spoke he continued to rummage through the file of envelopes of all sizes that were in the canister. "Now the one I am looking for arrived only two weeks back. I read it quickly as I do every letter that comes to me. One in a thousand might just have a connection to a crime worth my attention. I hadn't thought this one did. It came from a precocious child."

He continued to dig through yet another stack of letters. "Aha! Here it is. Yes. Posted from Canada three weeks ago. I must commend the Post Office on their efficiency. Here Watson, read it aloud to me. You will quite enjoy it."

I took the envelope from Holmes's hand, opened it and unfolded the letter. "The post mark is from Avonlea, P.E.I., Canada. P.E.I.? What is that?"

"Prince Edward Island. It is a part of Canada with no more people living in it than are in Tunbridge Wells but yet it is an entire province. It was named in honor of the father of Queen Victoria, whom she adored, not in honor of her son, our current king, whom she despised. It is no matter. Do read the letter itself."

"Very well," said I. "It is written in the hand of what I would guess is a young woman, possibly no more than a girl. Very well, here goes;

Dear Mr. Sherlock Holmes:

I am truly very sorry for bothering you with this letter but I lay awake all last night trying to think of what else I could do. I tried to think of what might be sensible and try as I might sending this letter to you is the only thing I could think of when I was trying my hardest to be sensible. I had made a solemn vow that I would not say a word about this to anyone on earth and a solemn vow should never be broken, but I reasoned, sensibly I hope, that you and I are kindred spirits. I know you are because I have read all about you in *The Strand* magazine that comes every month to our local library.

Marilla Cuthbert - she is my guardian but she loves me as much as any mother could ever love a daughter even if she is reticent to let on at times - will not permit me to read about detectives at home as she says that there is nothing profitable to be gained by such idle nonsense. I assume she is right and it may not be entirely forthcoming of me to read about you at the public library but I confess that I do so every month when *The Strand* appears and from those stories I have deduced that you are my kindred spirit. I know this because you place such great value on imagination. On numerous occasions in the stories about you that are written by Dr. Watson you have said that the men at Scotland Yard may be diligent and plodding policemen but they lack imagination. I have arrived at the same conclusion about most of the students in my class. Imagination is such a gift is it not? I am so fortunate that I have an imagination. Don't you feel the same way, Mr. Holmes?

So when I tell a secret to my kindred spirit I have explained to myself that it is really only as if I am telling something to myself and therefore not violating my solemn vow, but I must get on with my story. You tell your clients to state their case and so I will mine and I assure you that everything I say is factual and not in any way a creation of my imagination.

On the fifteenth day of June, that is two and a half months ago although it seems much less as the summer has passed so quickly, I attended the prize-giving assembly for the Avonlea Public School, held in the lovely ballroom of the White Sands Hotel, overlooking the Atlantic Ocean on the north shore of Prince Edward Island. The schedule of the evening was rather significant for me as I won the prize for both English Composition and English Literature although I only came a disappointing second in overall student achievement as a result of my receiving a lower grade in geometry, in which I am truly a dunce. I came second to another of my fellow students who it appears will be my

eternal nemesis and whose name I will not
speak, but as you are a detective I must be
honest in my communications with you and
admit that he is in truth a very clever
young man, as well as athletic, as well as
on the handsome side, and as well as tall,
and usually but not always well-mannered.

When all the prizes had been given out
and the entire assembly had stood and sung
"God Save the King" I took the few minutes I
knew I would have to myself to look out over
the ocean. It was a wondrous moonlit night
and the ocean was dappled as if with
diamonds, and I went all alone to the far
end of the long porch of the hotel that
allows an unobstructed view of the ocean so
that I might have just a few moments to
enjoy the rapturous feelings that come over
me when I look out over the sparkling
ripples. I was a little vexed to see that
there was another person standing in my
favorite spot on the porch and looking out
over the ocean as well. However, as it was
the summer time and there are always heaps
of Americans at the hotel I told myself that
I should not be selfish and I should share
my favorite place on the porch with this
other person and that, after all, I lived
close to the ocean and enjoyed this
opportunity many times and that this visitor
was most likely from a city and that it
would be an exceptionally special moment for
her. I say "her" because as I drew up beside

her I could see that she was a girl of about the same age and height as I although she was blessed with a fuller figure than mine, which is very much on the thin side, bordering on skinny, and she was wearing a dress of pale-pink organdy.

I came and stood quite close beside her as there is only a limited space in which one can obtain the best view of the ocean. She turned and looked at me and I was struck speechless, which is a condition, as Marilla will most assuredly tell you, that is entirely uncommon for me to experience. Such a thrill was going up and down my back. She, the other girl that is, likewise said nothing but the two of us continued to stare at each other for we could see that both of us were not only of the same age and height but both had flaming red hair. Hers was perhaps even brighter than mine which in my wildest imagination, which can be quite wild indeed, I could not have dreamed. For those who have not had to bear the cross of flaming red hair it is impossible to know what a burden it is to be so different from all the rest of the girls in your class and to be compared in a hurtful way to a carrot. When I saw her I knew immediately that she and I were kindred spirits as a result of our common tribulations. I extended my hand to her and said, "Hello. I am Anne Shirley." She replied, in a very polite way and with such a refined English accent, "I am very pleased to meet you Anne. I am Cordelia de la Mare." For a moment I was filled with envy that she should have such an elegant name, one that came close to what I had imagined I might have been called had I lived in a more romantic era, but I told myself to put away any envious or uncharitable thoughts as it was obvious that her hair was ever redder than mine, and that she had even more freckles than I do, and that while my nose and features could be called aquiline hers were definitely more Gaelic and so it was only right and fair that she should have a name that is far more elegant than mine and have a refined English accent, as I am sure that you and Dr. Watson do as well, do you not? Or are you Scottish?

In the much too short but oh so fascinating time that we had to converse with each other she told me that her aunt had brought her to the White Sands for the summer and that she would be leaving at the end of August. I asked her about her family and her parents and she told me that she did not have any living mother or father but that she was cared for by a loving guardian who treated her as if she was his own daughter.

Mr. Holmes, words cannot express the feelings I had in my heart as I listened to her. I told her that I too was an orphan and cared for by loving guardians. Then we just stood and looked at each other as if we were afraid that such a special moment of kinship would vanish if either were to utter a word. Then I heard Marilla calling for me to come for it was time to return to Green Gables, that being that name of my home, and so we both quite without warning threw our arms around each other and said goodbye and I told her that I would come to visit the next morning even if I had to walk the entire five miles.

I did not sleep at all that night as I had been thrown into a very distressing quandary. In my heart I knew that Cordelia was destined by fate to be my bosom friend but I already had a bosom friend, my dear Diana Barry to whom I was devoted and pledged, and it was not at all appropriate to have two bosom friends as that would lead to all sorts of jealousy and envy and unpleasantness. So in the middle of the night I looked up at the moon from my window in the east gable and said a little private but still interesting prayer for wisdom. Immediately that prayer was answered when I remembered, although I had not truly forgotten such an important matter but it had temporarily escaped by thinking in the intensity of the moment, that Diana had told me that she was going away for the summer to spend it with relatives on her father's side in Ontario. The wonderful realization came to me that while one should not have two bosom friends in the same place at the same time it was quite acceptable to have them sequentially and that Cordelia's arrival had been a gift to me from Providence in response to a yet unspoken prayer for a friend with whom to spend my summer vacation in Avonlea.

The summer proved to be a joyful experience for me and, except for some occasions which I will describe below, for Cordelia as well. She demonstrated an imagination every bit as vivid as mine and we resurrected the Story Club that Jane and Diana and Ruby and I had begun the previous summer but had ended in ignominy and humiliation when I came close to drowning and had to be rescued by the aforementioned young man who is still my eternal nemesis. I told her all about my imagined stories that were set in Lovers' Lane or by the shore of the Lake of Shining Waters, and she told me so many wonderful stories, some that she had been told and others from her own splendid imagination about knights and ladies of old and about King Arthur and Queen Guinevere and Sir Lancelot and Sir Gallahad. At first Marilla thought it a poor use of my time and chastised me for not doing my chores around the farm but Matthew, he is Marilla's brother and my other loving guardian, got up very early and drove me to the White Sands Hotel, and on other days Cordelia would have the carriage from the hotel deliver her to Green Gables and then she said that we could solve all of Marilla's objections if she were to help me with my chores. I thought this would be most ungracious and poor etiquette of me to have a friend come to visit and then to expect her to work and do chores that quite rightfully were mine but Cordelia was not only kind but eager to help as she had never lived on a farm and never been close to cows and horses and found it all quite exotic. I suppose that if you come from a genteel part of England then cows and horses might seem exotic though I confess I do not think of them in that manner.

Marilla at first pretended to find the two of us together to be, as she said, "double trouble" and said that she was constantly seeing twins and even more concerned for her eyesight which has not been strong for many years and gives her great headaches. But soon she stopped saying anything and wished only that Cordelia could stay for much longer.

Twice there were concerts in Charlottetown and all of my friends and even Josie Pye attended them along with Cordelia. Josie said she was complimenting Cordelia and me by saying that we looked like the healthiest patch of carrots she had ever seen, and of course this was not a compliment at all and I had to restrain myself from saying uncharitable things about Josie to Cordelia but she soon saw for

herself and made up her own mind about Josie
Pye.

I said that the summer was joyous,
except that on several occasions I happened
upon Cordelia and found her weeping. When
she saw me she immediately composed herself
and made as if all were well but I could
tell that she was deeply anxious and
distressed about something. The other quite
odd thing I observed was that whenever I
called her by name and she saw that I was
speaking to her she immediately responded to
me, but when we were in a group of people
and she was not looking at me she would just
ignore my calling her by name until I almost
had to shout it to get her attention. She is
most certainly not hard of hearing and it
was as if she did not recognize her own name
being spoken. I found these things very
perplexing but said nothing, except for once
in early July and then Cordelia acted as if
she were cross with me for speaking of such
things and so I said nothing more.

On the twenty-fifth day of August, just
a few days ago, the two of us, after all my
chores were finished, sat on the sand dunes
looking out over the ocean. It was a most
glorious day and to be there with my bosom
friend was a joy that thrilled me to the
depths of my soul. I spoke openly of my
affection for my friend and told her how
much I would miss her when she departed in a
few days. She broke into tears and could not

stop crying bitterly. Her whole body was wracked with sobs and she threw her arms around me and said over and over again, "I'm sorry. I'm so sorry. Please forgive me. I'm so sorry Anne" I held her as she cried for several minutes and then she finally composed herself and looked directly into my eyes and said, "My name is not Cordelia de la Mare, it is Belinda Murphy. My guardian, who has become my father, is John Openshaw of Coventry, England and I am here because I have been kidnapped and if I go to the police they will kill my father."

She then unburdened her heart and told me the most incredible heart-rending story. She said that she had been born in Georgia, in America, and that her parents had died of fever and left her as an orphan. She had lived in an orphanage in Savannah for two years before being adopted by Mr. and Mrs. Openshaw of Palm Beach County, Florida. She did not know fully what had happened that caused the death of Mrs. Openshaw and Mr. Openshaw Senior but she knew that it had been a tragedy and that foul play was possibly involved. Her father, Mr. Openshaw that is, who she referred to as her father, then took her to live in England where she had enjoyed a most pleasant and privileged life for over six years. England became her home and she loved going to a very esteemed school for girls and doing well in her studies and engaging in sports. She said that she even took the prize in geometry, which made me most envious as it has been the bane of my existence in Avonlea. But then on a winter day just prior to last Christmas some strangers called at her house while her father was away in town. They were a well-dressed couple who spoke with American accents and informed the maid that they were friends of Mr. Openshaw from Florida in America. The maid had no reason to doubt their word and so she invited them to wait in the parlor until Mr. Openshaw returned from town. But then another two men suddenly appeared from the carriage and came rushing into the house. They were large men and very nasty looking and one of them held the maid while the other two beat the hired man until he was unconscious. She said that she ran to her bedroom and locked the door but they kicked it down and came and grabbed her and held a cloth over her face. Most likely it was saturated with chloroform, not that I know anything about this but I have read about it in your detective stories. When she woke up she was on board a ship and locked in a cabin. The woman who had come to her door in Coventry then entered the cabin and told her, in a very cross way, that she could never say anything of what had happened or her father would be killed. The woman said her name was Morag and the Cordelia was to call her Aunt Morag. If she agreed to what they demanded then she would be allowed out of the cabin and might someday be returned to her father. She was terrified and remains so to this day.

The ship they were on reached America several days later at the port of Savannah and she was taken from there by train to St. Augustine. She remained there, confined to an estate home of a large plantation until the beginning of the summer. She was miserable but was too afraid to do anything for fear that they would kill her father. The same unpleasant woman lived there, the one called Aunt Morag, and she reminded her daily that both she and her father were being watched and that they would be tortured if they tried to break the conditions of their situation.

The house she was confined to was a meeting place for some very awful people. At night, after she had been sent to her room, she would sit at the top of the stairs and listen to her kidnapers and their visitors talk and say terrible things about negroes, and Catholics, and Jewish people. She heard how they had burned some of their homes, and even murdered some, and how they had made it look as if it were all by accident. She heard how they were expanding their secret organization all over America, and even into Canada and Mexico, and how they had spies and agents all over the world. It was then that she understood that these were the same people who had burned down her father's house years ago and killed the woman who would have become her mother, and the man who would have been her grandfather. She heard them speak about "the Klan" and she heard the words "Ku Klux Klan."

In June she was suddenly taken from St. Augustine and she and Aunt Morag and several of the men took a very long train journey and eventually they ended up in Prince Edward Island. She said she is not sure but she believes that this group of people had been given the assignment of establishing the evil organization in Canada. Aunt Morag was not at all happy about it and complained many times that she was being sent to some god-forsaken corner of some primitive country. But the White Sands Hotel became their secret headquarters. They stayed there because it is very out-of-the-way and I guess no one would suspect that anyone who ever stayed there could ever even think of doing anything truly nasty. But as I said before, there were heaps of Americans coming and going all summer and there were many meetings in the cottage that she was forced to stay in.

She said that her life had become a perfect graveyard as one hope after another was buried, but my coming into her life was a godsend and that every night in her prayers she thanked God for sending me. There have been one or two times when Marilla has said something similar and it makes me feel rather embarrassed and guilty because I know that I should never let myself give in to vanity, but that is truly what she said.

Surely, Mr. Holmes, you can imagine that hearing this story from her shocked me to the depths of my soul. I had thought all along that there was something very odd and strange about Cordelia, but then there are many people in Avonlea who think that I am sometimes odd and strange, and if she had been an orphan as I had been then I concluded that it was normal that orphans could be expected to exhibit behavior that others who were never orphans, let alone those who had never had the burden of red hair, could not understand.

I told Cordelia, who I now had to think of as Belinda, which is still a pleasant name but nowhere near as romantic as Cordelia, that she must forgive me but how could I believe all that she was saying. Such things were even beyond my imagination. While some people, Josie Pye would come to mind, and the entire Pye family for that matter, are at times not always pleasant and considerate of others' feelings, no one in Avonlea or indeed anyone I have met on the island, would ever think to burn down someone's house, or kill them just because they went to a different church, which is not to say that all of our Baptists are always completely charitable to our Methodists, but none would ever seek to do

34

harm. I might have imagined that in the Haunted Woods there could be found the ghost of a murdered child, but I did not exactly believe that, and certainly not during the daytime. So I said to Cordelia that I was having some difficulty believing everything she had told me and I was wondering how much of it was truly true and how much was imagination. That she had grown up in England I could believe because of her lovely refined English accent, but the being kidnapped by the Ku Klux Klan and taken to Florida, and being privy to all these things and people that were coming and going from Florida and the Deep South of the United States, well that was asking me to believe a lot even from a red haired girl who had become by bosom friend, at least for the summer.

She just nodded and told me to wait a minute and went back to her cottage. She returned forthwith carrying a small bag and she gave it to me. "Here," she said. "These arrived just days ago with our most recent visitors." I looked inside and there were five of the most perfect, large, round oranges I have ever seen in my life. Occasionally at Christmas time boys and girls might receive an orange and an apple in their Christmas stockings, but never any as perfect at these were. And every one of them had the word 'FLORIDA' stamped in ink on their perfect orange skin. "These are for you and Matthew and Marilla. I have been eating them all summer long. You can see they came from Florida."

Cordelia, who had now become Belinda, made me swear a very solemn oath that I could never tell anyone, not even Marilla and Matthew, the things she had told me, and that she had only told me because she loved me as her bosom friend and had no other friends at all in the entire world, and she could not bear to think that she would be leaving in a day and might never see me again, and that she would have to live for the rest of her life knowing that my affection for her was based on a lie.

She said that Aunt Morag had agreed to let her send me letters, much as she had sent them to her father, on the condition that nothing could ever be revealed about her secret life, and every letter would be inspected before it could be sent. Very quickly I imagined that we could use a secret code in our letters and circumvent the censorious Aunt Morag. I had that idea because I remembered reading the Sherlock Holmes mystery about the dancing men and the way that messages were given by secret code. Together we came up with the idea to using the first letter of every sentence we would write to say things in secret. Do you think that was a good idea for a secret code, Mr. Holmes? Aunt Morag is not exactly the sharpest knife in the drawer, as Marilla might say about some of the people in Avonlea, and I do not believe that she will discover our secret.

The next day Cordelia did not come to Green Gables in the morning as she had been doing and in the afternoon I asked Matthew to take me to White Sands. When we arrived at the hotel I asked and was told that Cordelia and her party had checked out of the hotel the evening before, and that they had no forwarding address except for a mail service in New York City. My heart was broken not just because I would never, I believed, see my dear friend again, but because I had not even had the opportunity to share parting hugs with her and to cry together, which is such a beautifully painful thing for two girls to do together when both of their hearts are broken.

It was the most tragical thing that had ever happened to me. For two days I tossed and turned in my bed at night and was totally distracted, even more than usual according to Marilla. I couldn't eat anything because my heart was broken, and eating even Marilla's good boiled pork and greens is so unromantic which one is in affliction.

Then the solution came to me - the idea of unburdening my heart to you, who as I have said already I had known to be my kindred spirit. And so I have sent you this letter. I do hope that you will not think that I have rambled on far too long, as I am wont to do in my stories, and that you will not think that I am just a silly girl from Canada who has an imagination that is beyond imagining, as Marilla might say.

If you are to respond to me, and I do hope in my heart that you will for you are my only hope for Cordelia, who is now Belinda, and may I implore you to communicate with me through Miss Josephine Barry of Dominion Street in Charlottetown with the instructions that the letters and telegrams are for "that Anne girl." She is a very upright lady who is somewhat fond of me as long as I do not jump on top of her while she is asleep in a spare bedroom. I have no possible way of paying for your services as a consulting detective but Cordelia who is now Belinda said that her father is a wealthy man and I know that he would reward you most handsomely if you were able to restore his daughter to him

Thank you, Mr. Holmes, for considering this request and I remain,

Respectfully yours,

Anne Shirley

P.S. Please note that my name is Anne, with an "e"

3 TO CANADA

"Holmes," said I, putting down the many pages of the letter. "This is a most unusual story. Do you believe that it could be true? This is all from the hand of a young woman who is not much more than a child. Surely you are not going to drop your other cases and journey to Canada, of all places, to intervene."

"Most certainly I am," he replied, and then added with a smile, "and you, my dear doctor are coming with me. The other cases in my docket can be put aside, as can your patients. A case has been presented to us that involves murder most gruesome, and more than one; deeds most foul, kidnapping, lives in dangers, secret criminal societies, a distraught English father, and not one but two young people who have the gift of imagination. Did you really think for a moment that I would turn it down?"

"No," I replied, with a sigh. I got up from my chair and made my way to my bedroom. "I will pack and be ready by the morning."

"Ah, and would you be so kind as to check the schedule for the next steamship to America, and book us passage on whichever is the fastest one. And oh, a lecture tour might be a plausible reason for our visit and not arouse suspicions."

"Certainly, Holmes. Good night Holmes."

* * *

As good fortune would have it, the *RMS Lusitania* was in Liverpool and scheduled to depart to Boston and then New York in three days. Earlier in the year it had held the *Blue Riband*, having set a new record for a transatlantic crossing of just four days and sixteen hours. I secured tickets for us on the Upper Deck, courtesy of Mr. John Openshaw, and hastily we made plans for our journey. Unlike our previous voyage to the New World, which had been in glorious weather conditions, this crossing, in the midst of the equinoctial gales was a rough one. The Cunard Lines had determined to offer the fastest service across the ocean and kept the ship steaming at twenty-five knots for the entire crossing. The speed combined with the swells brought the spray and wash from the ocean constantly over the decks and none of the passengers were so foolish as to venture out into the open. Holmes and I stayed in our state rooms for almost the entire journey, leaving only for meals in the dining room. Sherlock Holmes was now quite a famous personage in England, and indeed throughout the world, thanks to my stories about him in *The Strand* and, in America, in *Collier's* magazines. He had no use for public recognition or adulation and when venturing outside of our cabin went disguised as a clergyman. While simple it was adequate for deceiving the rest of the passengers.

Throughout the voyage he busied himself with reading the masses of files that had been supplied to him by his brother Mycroft.

"This Ku Klux Klan is far more powerful than I had ever imagined, Watson," he said one morning over breakfast. "Thousands of veterans of the Confederate Army joined up following the War Between the States and it appears that they and their offspring have continued to keep in contact with each other since then. As soon as Mr. Openshaw's cases files arrived in the bowels of Whitehall, Mycroft sent his minions to work on them, all those nameless faceless bureaucrats who took firsts at Oxford and Cambridge and now believe they are advancing the progress of the human race by working for the British government."

"Hmm," I replied. "He must have thought the matter important."

"Indeed he did," replied Holmes. "Even though the files are several decades old the names of several score of agents of the Klan who are active in England were found therein. Most are still living and all are now being put under discreet surveillance. He has had the entire contents summarized and put into a document that he is prepared to wire to the American Department of Justice for their action. I constrained him to hold off on doing so, as it would jeopardize our efforts on behalf of our client, and might even put lives at risk. He has agreed to my request but not for more than one month's duration. We will have no time to waste once we land in Boston."

Around noon of our fifth day at sea we entered the inner harbor of Boston, Massachusetts. As I looked to the north I could see the large scar of burned buildings that had been incinerated in the Great Chelsea Fire of a few months earlier. The North Side, where we docked, had escaped the fire completely and was alive with hustle and bustle. The majority of the passengers remained on board, destined to New York City and a new life in America. Holmes and I departed and hailed a motorized taxicab to take us to Copley Square.

"Welcome to Baawston, gentlemen," said the driver as he pulled away from the docklands. "Do you have taxicayabs like this in Lawndon? We call them 'hummingbawds' 'cause of their noiyse, but they do the job." Indeed the vehicle did make a continuous humming sound as it worked its way along Atlantic Avenue, and Boylston Street and eventually to the grand Copley Square Hotel.

"I say, Holmes," said I. "We could take in some American history whilst we are here. The house belonging to Paul Revere is only a few blocks away. Should we go and see it?" His answer was exactly what I expected.

"I have no interest in commemorating one of the greatest blunders of history. Had the impetuous colonists remained in the Empire they would have had their own responsible government soon enough, ended slavery nearly a century before they did and avoided a civil war that killed or maimed a million young men."

Sherlock Holmes was not a fan of the history of the colony that got away.

If I could not enjoy any of the city's historical attractions I was determined at least to partake of the excellent seafood. The dining room of the hotel was serving fresh lobster that had been brought into the port earlier the same day. It was a crackling fine dinner.

Sherlock Holmes did not enjoy dining that required one to wrestle with crustaceans and settled for the steamed halibut. He ate in silence as he read and re-read several long telegrams from Mycroft that were waiting for us at the hotel.

Without looking up from his papers he informed me that, "Mycroft's agents have told him that this malicious Klan organization has steadily expanded into New England and has become rather successful in recruiting members in the towns west of Boston and even as far north as Maine."

"I thought they were opposed to giving rights to the negroes," I said. "Other than a few of the porters at the dock and the hotel I have hardly seen any darker skinned chaps in Boston. And surely there cannot be any of them up in Maine."

"The Klan," said Holmes, "is not just opposed to sharing America with those with dark skin; they apparently also have it in for immigrants from Ireland and Italy, the Jews and all the French-Canadian Catholics who have migrated to New England. They are demanding 'America for Americans' and setting up local organizations across the country. It may be many years before the sensible people of this country rid themselves of their peculiar cancer."

He said nothing more that evening and I retired to a finely appointed room to get a good night's sleep.

We were up very early the following morning and off to the train station. The Canadian Pacific Railway had extended service to Boston and we boarded their seven o'clock northbound train.

"Wasn't this the railroad that Peter Carey had shares in, Holmes?" I asked, thinking back to a case that Holmes had solved in '95, a rather gruesome one involving the impaling of a chap on a harpoon, "Yes, "responded Holmes. "John Neligan's father had purchased them many years earlier. By the time they were stolen by Black Peter and finally recovered by Neligan they were worth a small fortune. Let us hope that the CPR's punctuality and service live up to its share price."

I had not fully informed Sherlock Holmes of the itinerary I had booked with Thomas Cook. I reasoned that if I were to come all the way to some sparsely populated corner of Canada then at least I could arrange a detour to see one of the lovely Canadian settings by the ocean, and I had arranged an overnight in the famous Algonquin Hotel, the grand castle-like resort in St. Andrews By-the-Sea. It had opened just a few years earlier and was renowned for being a favorite of royalty, heads of state, captains of industry, and famous actors and musicians. Its golf course, with the spectacular views of the ocean, was reputed to be one of the most visually appealing in the world.

Sherlock Holmes did not engage in golf.

Upon arrival at the station in St. Andrews I announced that we were getting off. Holmes looked at me, rather puzzled and demanded, "Why in the deuce are we getting off now? It is no more than mid day. Surely we can make better use of our time and keep going until nightfall."

I feigned helplessness and blamed it on the travel agent and innocently asked, "They have a golf course and would rent you a set of clubs. Would you be interested in a round?"

"Nothing but 'A good walk, spoiled'", scoffed Holmes, quoting Mr. Twain. "But the place does appear to have a rather fine long veranda upon which I can consume several pipes and contemplate this case, while you, my good doctor, amuse yourself upon the links."

Amuse and enjoy myself I did. I had seen some paintings of the eastern Canadian forests in the autumn but had never looked out over such a magnificent canvas of glorious color as I observed that day. The reds, and golds, and purples, and browns, all mingled together with the enormous evergreens made a sight that I will never forget. I was matched up with three other gentlemen, one American and two Canadians who thankfully were every bit as much duffers on the course as I was. I made the mistake of signing in under my true name of Dr. John Watson and immediately one of them asked if I were related to that chap who wrote all those Sherlock Holmes stories. I confessed that I was and became quite the celebrated new friend of the three of them. I had hoped to discreetly sound them out about the activities of the Ku Klux Klan but thought I had foolishly lost that opportunity, as any hint that Sherlock Holmes had come to Canada to investigate the activities of the Klan could have put our client's daughter at risk if word got back to the villains who were holding her. And we knew right well that they had their spies everywhere.

At the rest stop after the ninth hole I decided to try my best at extracting information in the manner I had seen Sherlock Holmes do so often and so effectively; by pretending that I really did not want to know and challenging whatever it was they told me.

"So I hear that the towns up and down New England are all being flooded with immigrants from all over the world but that everyone is getting along quite famously and all are treated as equals," I said to the American chap.

Before he could answer the first Canadian fellow chipped in with, "That's not what we hear. If you can believe what we read in our papers there's everybody at everybody else's throat every weekend. Those from Germany don't like the Greeks, the French from France don't like the French from Quebec, nobody likes the Irish, and those of English stock think they own the whole country and were intended by God to rule over the rest of the world."

"And in Canada? No problems like that here?" I asked, all innocence.

"No sir," replied the second Canadian. "We're all for peace, order and good government and we all get along, no matter where in the world you've come from. That's the Canadian way, eh?"

To this remark the American chap smiled and responded, "Well now, we have had a few problems handling all those millions of folks from around the world who keep coming to America to start a new life. I guess they see us as the promised land. It makes sense that you wouldn't have the same problems in Canada since nobody wants to come here. Really, how many folks have moved to Canada in the past ten years? A thousand?"

Eager not to let any nationalistic differences emerge I changed the subject, "At least neither New England nor Canada is like those strange places in the South where those devils in bed sheets and dunce caps go riding around making life miserable for new comers and negroes."

"You mean the Klan?" responded the American. "No sir, you don't see them out at night in New England. Not yet. But they're here. I've heard tell of them setting up secret local groups all over Massachusetts, New Hampshire and Maine. They hear that the negroes are on the move from the South and coming to the factories of the North and those Klan fellows are determined to make them feel real unwelcome. Yes, sir. Sad to say. But they're here all right."

"And in Canada?" I said, again turning to the two Canadian chaps. "You wouldn't have any of those devils in Canada now would you?"

"No sir," replied both of the Canadians in unison. "If one of those blackguards ever showed his face north of the border he would be chased right back across. No sir. Never had any of those fellows around these parts."

"And proud you should be of that," said the American, again with a sly smile. "Of course you never had any issues about miscegenation of the races since you only ever had one race here. Not difficult to be more than good and fair to the negroes when there aren't any to be found in the country."

"Now there sir," snapped the first Canadian, "is where you are wrong. We don't have near as many as you have but we have a goodly number all right. Several thousand living in Halifax as we speak."

"Indeed," I replied, as I had not known this fact either.

"Yes sir. First batch came after the American Revolution. Came with the Loyalists they did. Of course they were slaves of the loyalists when they were in America, but the moment the set foot on Canadian soil they were free men and women. Yes sir, they were. Another whole lot came after the war we had with the Yankees around 1812 to 1814. The British government told the American slaves that they could have freedom and free land in Canada if they would come and fight for our side. So heaps of them did. And then we had another lot arrive on what they called the Underground Railroad before your Civil War and before Abe Lincoln set them all free. So yes sir. We have a whole town of them, Africville they call it, right up against Halifax. Nice little community with their own pretty small houses and schools and church and all. There's quite a few of them there. And lots more in other villages all though the Maritimes, sir."

"Yeah," responded the American. "I do recall hearing about that place, Africville. Yeah. In the United States of America we would call a place like that where we make all the negroes live 'a slum.' So tell me what did you call it in Canada? A 'community'? Now that is rich isn't it? I'll have to let our negro folks know that they're not living in a slum, they're in a community." I think it took all the fellow's self-control not to break out laughing.

"Very well, sir, you may mock us, but at least we do not plant burning crosses on their lawns and burn them out of their homes. Your American Klansmen are not permitted on Canadian soil."

"You're lucky," responded the American. "Just you wait."

"Right!" I announced, before anyone else could say anything. "I see the tenth green is open so let us get on with the game."

We finished the game, making an unspoken pact to talk about nothing except drivers, and irons and putters. After the eighteenth hole we all shook hands and parted. I returned to the long veranda of the Algonquin to find Holmes where I had left him, reading his stack of papers and smoking on his beloved pipe. I passed along what little I had gleaned from my fellow golfers. He said nothing for several minutes and then, "We have an early train to catch tomorrow morning. I suggest that we dine early, my good doctor." With that he rose and walked towards the dining room. I followed.

4 AND THEN TO AVONLEA

The following morning we did indeed rise early, well before six o'clock. The hotel provided a breakfast in a box for us to take with us on the train and we departed for the station. By the end of the morning, after two changes of trains, we arrived at the small port of Cape Tormentine on the east coast of the province of New Brunswick. Tied to the pier was a large wooden steamboat, *The Stanley*. We boarded and prepared for the crossing.

Compared to the luxury of the *Lusitania*, the vessel we found ourselves on was closer to *Noah's Ark*, with two of every known life form crammed on board. There were small clusters of upper class gents and ladies in fine attire, dark skinned Canadian Indians, farmers, tradesmen of every sort, stevedores, salesmen, clergy, earnest looking young women who I guessed might be teachers, and a doctor and two nurses. In addition there were cows, and sheep, and pigs, and chickens, and pallets laden with sacks of flour, sugar, corn meal and countless other items whose contents I could not begin to guess. This boat was the lifeline to the island and everything that came and went had to get on and off *The Stanley*.

49

Fortunately the crossing only took a couple of hours, and we arrived at the port of Borden by the late afternoon. The good folks at Thomas Cook had booked seats for us on the Prince Edward Island Railroad, which had a spur running all the way to the dockside. I thought it odd that such a small population could afford a full service railway system, but there it was and so we boarded.

By now it was early evening and the sun was low in the western sky. I found myself fascinated by the landscape that was passing us. The small roads were cut into the red clay soil, barely wide enough for two carriages to pass each other. The houses were not much more than cottages, and the barns looked as if they had been built for pygmies. It did not look like a wealthy province, but neither did it look poor. It was just so very neat and quaint. Then it struck me. It looked like those paintings I had seen of the English countryside in the era of Queen Elizabeth. It was almost as if we had been transported to a land that time forgot, a lost world that unlike those of Rider Haggard was neither exotic nor fearsome. Neither Allan Quatermain nor She-who-must-be-obeyed were going to come to rescue us. The entire place exuded a quiet sense of safety. Suddenly I felt that Holmes and I must have arrived on the wrong planet, searching for murderous villains who could not possibly be imagined to inhabit this quaint little corner of the globe.

After less than a half an hour we pulled into the station at a whistle-stop named Bright River and got off the train. From here, if the good travel agents had done their job, we would be met by one of the local yeomen who picked up and delivered travelers on their way to the north shore and the White Sands Hotel.

The three other passengers who alighted from the train with us were met by small carriages and departed, quickly disappearing out of sight beyond the gently rolling green hills of this strange little world. There was no one in sight that looked as if they might be waiting for a fare and I was quite sure that if I shouted at the top of my lungs for a taxi I would be only making a fool of myself in front of the circling sea gulls. So Holmes and I sat on a bench and waited. Twilight fell and the temperature dropped. Holmes and I looked at each other and suddenly he began to laugh. He laughed so seldom that I was pleased to join in although I had no idea whatsoever as to the source of his amusement. Shaking his head, he turned to me and spoke.

"My dear doctor, my friend, is it not the height of absurdity that England's finest, howbeit only, consulting detective and one of its most famous authors find themselves in the middle of nowhere wondering if anyone will come to fetch them, and worried that we might catch our death of cold if we have to wait here until the morning train arrives to rescue us. It is utterly humbling, and I suppose a good thing for the soul. Would you not agree?"

"I would indeed, Holmes. Mind you I could better manage the humble part if I thought that sometime before daybreak someone would provide at least a hot cup of tea and some supper. We have grown frightfully dependent on Mrs. Hudson."

"Next time, Watson, you shall bring her with us."

"Next time, Holmes? Pray tell me, I do not believe you have let me in on that data yet."

Holmes laughed again, and we both shook our heads and kept looking down the road.

It was close to twenty minutes after the train had departed that I saw the faint glow of a carriage lantern bobbing its way up and down in the distance. Soon I could hear the clip-clop of a slow horse and finally an open carriage, more like a farm wagon with benches in the back, pulled into to road side of the station. It was pulled by an old sorrel mare that I knew had not galloped in over a decade, and a roughly dressed barrel-chested gentleman of about sixty years of age got out and shuffled towards us.

"Mr. Holmes and Dr. Watson," he said, looking at our luggage and not at our faces.

"Indeed," said Holmes. "The same. And you are the livery service to the White Sands I trust?"

He made no reply but tossed our steamer trunks and valises into the wagon, pointed at the step that we had to use to climb inside, and once we were seated, he climbed up to the driver's seat.

"Well now," he said, directing his speech to the back end of the mare, but loud enough for Holmes and I to hear. "I dunno. I s'pose that's what I must be tonight, seein' as there's nobody else on the road, and I the only one picking you up. Yes, I s'pose that's what I must be." After that he was silent.

A few minutes later Holmes spoke again. "I gather the train arrived somewhat earlier than usual."

There was no reply for nearly a minute. Then, "Well now, I dunno. It arrived at the same time it's been arriving for over thirty years, so I don't s'pose it was early. Unless of course they changed the train schedule this morning, and wanted it to arrive later. Maybe they did that, in which case it would be early as you say, sir. I dunno." This statement was followed by another stretch of silence.

"Is it very far to the hotel?" asked Holmes.

"Well now," came the reply. "It wouldn't be very far if'n I had a faster horse. Then it wouldn't be very far at all. But seeing as I only have this one then I guess it's pretty far. It'll take us at least another twenty minutes to get there.

Holmes shook his head, pulled out his pipe, packed and lit it and admitted defeat in the matter of conversation.

I continued to enjoy the night air and the brilliant display of stars overhead. I had never seen as many of them. In London, of course, you are lucky if you can see the moon what with all the smoke and light. But even in the Lake District I could not imagine seeing such a vast display of the heavens. As the wagon rounded a corner a flat dark stretch appeared in front of us, and I saw that we were looking at a large pond. We pulled out from under the cover of the tree branches and suddenly the surface of the lake was alive with silvery ripples as the glow of the moon dappled the tops of the tiny waves that had been stirred to life by the breeze blowing in from the sea.

To my surprise Holmes not only starred intensely at it but stood up and climbed into the seat beside the driver. Such an action was most unusual for him and I looked at him without saying a word.

"I must say sir," I heard him say to the chap who was driving us. "I am not one for amusing myself concerning the beauty of nature, but the vision in front of us is truly stunning. The waters of the lake appear to be shining, as if they possess a source of light all of their own and turned it on so that we should pause and enjoy the peacefulness and loveliness of this place."

"Well now, sir. It's truly interesting that you should say that." He paused and said nothing as we drove around the edge of the lake. "It was just over five years ago that I picked up our young girl from the train station and rode her along this same route and darned if she did not say just about the same thing as you did. I've lived here all my life and only saw this as Barry's Pond but she said that such a name was completely lacking in imagination and she called it the Lake of Shining Waters. So it's curious that your imagination worked the same way. She might decide that England's most famous detective is a kindred spirit. And then sir, well, then you just don't know how your whole life might change if she decides that, sir."

Overhearing his words, I spoke up. "You appear to know who we are sir."

"Well now, doctor. I'm guessing that everybody in Avonlea knows who you are. We get a heap of Americans come to the hotel in the summer, but to have the detective and writer that everybody has heard about arrive here at the end of September, well now that's quite special. Of course, Mrs. Rachel Lynde has made sure everyone in Avonlea knows about you coming here and I s'pose that most of the village will be hanging around the hotel when you arrive pretending that they're there for your lecture but they'll really just be there to be able to say that they saw you first and then that'll keep them talking about it for weeks; talking about what you were wearing, and what you looked like, and of course, the big thing is that they'll all be talking about what in heaven's name you are doing here in Avonlea. Now don't you mind them. They'll all be pretending that they don't know who you are and won't say nothing at all to you. They'll just want to be looking at you. So don't be worried about them."

There was another long pause and then he added, "Not that it's any of my concern sir, but you might think about just telling folks why you're here in Avonlea right off. Otherwise by morning there will be hundred reasons for you're being here and I would be pretty sure that a hundred and one of them will be wrong."

Here I spoke up again with the lines I had rehearsed. "Mr. Sherlock Holmes and I are indeed on a lecture and speaking tour of North America, sent by *The Strand* and *Harper's* magazines so that they can sell many more copies of their publications. And what better place to start than the eastern edge of Canada, from whence we will start to work our way clockwise over the entire continent."

"That so?" he replied, and then paused. "That seems a little surprising. Your magazine fellows must not be the sharpest knives in the drawer then."

"Why do you say that?" I countered, a bit taken aback that my well thought-out story was not immediately accepted.

"Well now, sir. It's just that those of us who can read don't have any money to use buying magazines and books. And those who can't read, well, they have even less money. So trying to sell magazines in the villages of Prince Edward Island just doesn't seem like a very smart idea, that's all."

CRAIG STEPHEN COPLAND

5 THE NEWEST IRREGULAR

By the time we approached the hotel darkness had overtaken us. The White Sands Hotel appeared in the distance like something out of a fairytale. Paper lanterns with small lights inside them had been strung along the walkways and under the long roof that hung out over the veranda. All of the windows were lighted and there was a small string quartet playing somewhere in the interior of the building with the strains of Barcarolle just barely perceptible over the sound of the surf rolling on to the beach behind the building. Sherlock Holmes, who as I have already noted, does not indulge in many sensual pleasures at the best of times cocked his head to listen more closely, and he smiled.

There were, as our driver had warned us, well over a hundred guests milling about on the lawn and the veranda. As we approached they moved with purposeful nonchalance closer to the driveway. Several of the hotel staff boys in crisp white shirts and green vests appeared and lifted our trunks and valises from the back of the wagon and took them inside. Holmes and I descended from the rustic carriage and made our way to the front desk.

"Welcome Mr. Sherlock Holmes and Dr. John Watson," beamed the desk manager. "We have been expecting you and we are all looking forward to your reading and lecture this evening. As time is of the essence we have your dinner waiting for you, so if it is acceptable to you please join us in the dining room."

The dining area was a large plain room at the rear of the hotel but its back wall was entirely windows and it looked out over the ocean – a rather pleasant spot I must say. We had barely been seated than the waiters brought us bowls of quite delicious hot seafood chowder. Holmes continued to smile. No sooner had we devoured them than the chaps appeared again with platters of their prized oversized crustacean. There were arranged so that the head of the beastly little thing starred directly at you, with his beady eyes fixed on whoever was about to devour him. The massive claws were laid in front of the head, with one claw well in front of the other as if reaching out to shake your hand. The thorax was splayed out at the back of the platter. Encircling the beast's body were wedges of what once must have been monstrous potatoes, and sections of corn, still on the cob.

Holmes was no longer smiling.

With stiff upper lip both of us managed to separate the ugly critter's flesh from his exoskeleton and eat him. Several looks passed between Holmes and me as we wrestled with our dinner and wondered how long it would be before we were once again able to enjoy a good steak and kidney pie, or fish and chips with mushy peas.

With no time to spare we were ushered into the hotel's ballroom as soon as we had laid down our dessert forks. Holmes was a seasoned perhaps even jaded lecturer and, given his distaste for having to crack open his dinner before eating it, not in the best of moods as he entered the hall. The reception however was more than pleasant. The entire room rose to their feet and gave us a warm round of applause as we walked towards our seats. The smiles were genuine and I permitted myself a moment of smug satisfaction knowing that my stories of the accomplishments of Sherlock Holmes had reached this otherwise forgotten corner of the Empire.

The hotel manager, who also covered the role of maitre d' in the dining room, strode to the podium and motioned the crowd to be seated and silent. Rather than introducing Holmes himself he called upon a tall handsome young man to do so. The lad had taken the top prize for overall academic achievement the year before in the local school and so to him the honor was given of introducing the famous visitor.

The young student rose and I noted that he was a fine looking boy, tall and lean, and with a fine set of dark curls on the top of his head. He firmly grasped the sides of the lectern and delivered an excellent introduction to Sherlock Holmes. He made sufficient passing references to the stories that I had written to demonstrate his masterful knowledge of the subject but not in a way that rendered him proud or boastful. His voice was clear and confident and I could not help imagining that he would make a fine teacher someday. As he concluded his speech and welcomed Holmes to the lectern I allowed myself a self-indulgent thought that indeed the young lad showed such promise that he might even become a doctor someday.

Holmes gave his polished lecture. He began, as he always did, by warning the listeners that as his subject was crime and the pursuit if dastardly criminals. As he would be providing some rather explicit details from some nefarious criminal acts, any in the audience who might be of a delicate disposition should feel free to depart now or at any time during the lecture, and that their so doing would be entirely understood. Of course no one got up to leave. No one ever did. They all were simply drawn to pay close attention with the expectation of titillation while feigning serious detached interest for the sake of science and the advancement of civilized society.

He did not disappoint. He never did. Without the need of a single note he delivered his talk – *The Science of Deduction* – and interspersed an abundance of forensic knowledge and the latest research in the field with salacious details of the crimes of Jack the Ripper and, for the specific interest of this audience, a rather full account of the evil Dr. Thomas Neill Cream, a Canadian who had studied at McGill University before going on to poison a host of men and women, including several prostitutes, both in Canada and subsequently in England. Numerous gasps of horror were heard from some of the ladies present but none fainted, knowing that by allowing themselves to do so they would miss out on the next revelation of horror that might stir their blood.

After his lecture ended I rose and recited one of my favorite stories about the exploits of Sherlock Holmes, *The Man with the Twisted Lip*. I was rather fond of this story as it led the reader to believe that murder most foul had been committed upon a young husband and father. His desperate and beautiful wife had sought the help of Sherlock Holmes, only to find that no crime had occurred at all. The young man was safe all along but had gone to bizarre depths of deceit in order to provide a good life for his much-loved wife and children. My reading of it always left the audience with rather warm feelings and a tear or two in the eyes of the young wives who were present and no doubt imagining that they were as loved by their husbands as Mrs. Neville St.Clair had been by hers.

After the warm applause had ended, the audience dispersed quite rapidly. It was getting late and most of these good folks were faming people, and it did not matter at what time they went to bed for the night the cows still demanded to be looked after at dawn. Once I was free of well-wishers I took myself out to the veranda and walked to the far end where one could have an unobstructed view of the open ocean. In the soft light from the lamps and lanterns I saw that someone else had had the same idea. I observed from behind that a tall, lithe, young woman stood facing the railing. Her hair, which cascaded down over her shoulders was a rich red in color. Her dress, tan in color, was cinched at the waist with a ribbon. The sleeves were puffed.

I stood beside her and together we admired the shimmering path of moonlight that flowed from the shore to the horizon.

"Good evening, Dr. Watson."

"Good evening, Anne."

"I most thoroughly enjoyed your story, and Mr. Holmes lecture was positively intoxicating. It struck to the very heart of my imagination and while listening all I could do was to pretend inside my mind that someday I would also be a great detective. It must be such a privilege for you to be able to help him and then to tell the rest of the world about him through all of your fascinating stories."

"Indeed it is Anne, but I am quite sure that while listening to us your mind was on other matters far more important."

With this she turned and looked at me and I found myself looking into the face of an adolescent young woman who was at one and the same time wise beyond her years, and yet still an exuberant and joyful child.

"You are entirely correct, sir," she said in a quiet serious tone. "I cannot thank you enough for reading my letter and believing in me and coming all the way to Avonlea to help save the life of my bosom friend, Belinda. I have been sore distressed for weeks since she revealed her situation to me, and your arrival is a godsend."

"As soon as Sherlock Holmes heard the full story of what was taking place," I assured her, "there was no power on earth that could keep him from coming here. He is grateful to you for imparting all the details to him. He will want to speak to you directly of course, and as soon as possible. Could you come back here to the hotel tomorrow morning? It will be Saturday so I do not believe it would interfere with your school day."

"Oh yes," Anne replied promptly. "As soon as I finish my chores Matthew will drive me over. You already met Matthew, did you not? It was he who greeted you at the train station and drove you here."

"Ah yes," I said. "I rather suspected that that was who he was, but he did not introduce himself. A bit on the shy side, I gather."

"Oh terribly, but as soon as he learned that you and Sherlock Holmes needed to be picked up at Bright River he said that he would come and get you. He knows how much a fan I am. Actually so are all my friends. We are enraptured of Sherlock Holmes and your stories. So yes sir, most certainly sir, I shall be here tomorrow morning by no later than ten o'clock."

"Very good then my dear," said I. "Allow me to bid you good night and be assured that both Sherlock Holmes and I will be eager to speak with you and place ourselves at the service of Belinda and her family."

"Yes. Good night, sir. But please give this to Sherlock Holmes." She removed a folded piece of paper that had been held under the ribbon of her dress and handed it to me. "It arrived just yesterday from Belinda. Mr. Holmes will want to read it. I am sure he will deduce the message that is hidden in it. Good night sir."

With that she turned and walked along the veranda and down the steps towards the waiting farm wagon. I watch her in silence and thanked Providence for the existence of such a remarkable girl.

6 ACCOMPANIED TO HALIFAX

I rose the following morning at dawn and made my way to the dining room. Beyond the windowed wall I could see a stone patio lying between the hotel and the embankment that marked the farthest reach of the sand beach. There were several tables and chairs on the patio and at one of them I saw none other than Sherlock Holmes, his head and legs covered by the hotel's blankets, his hunting hat on his head and a pipe in his mouth. I took a couple of blankets myself from the pile at the patio door and joined him in the cool, brisk but exhilarating air of the seaside.

"Ah, good morning, Watson," he said looking up from the local newspaper. "And how was your conversation in the moonlight with the newest member of the Baker Street Irregulars?"

I knew better than to bother asking him how he knew about my chat with Anne so I withheld my response and handed him the paper that she had given me as we parted. "Here Holmes. You need to read this."

"My dear doctor," Holmes responded. "You can see that I am already occupied with tea, the newspaper, and my pipe and have no hands left to hold a document. Pray indulge me and read it to me, if you don't mind."

"Very well Holmes," said I. "It is a letter from Miss Belinda Openshaw, the daughter of your client, to Anne Shirley. It is dated Sunday, September 27 and arrived here, according to Anne, two days ago, on Thursday, the first of October, and it reads:

My dearest Anne:

I hope this letter finds you well. Are you indeed well? Maybe you have not been well. I would hope not. Not that you ever get sick. Has anything been worrying you? Anne, you mustn't worry about school. Low marks have never crossed your path. I am back in school. Foreign languages are for me a challenge. Are they for you sometimes? Xenophon and other Greeks are killing me. Is Greek on your course? Are you studying Latin? Today we have a test in Greek. Tomorrow will be Latin. Even if I study hard, I am worried. Never have I had to work so much. Do you have to work for geometry? So do I. I also have to work hard in arithmetic. Reading however is a joy. Joy indeed is what I feel. On top of that is composition. How I loved the stories we composed together. Now I have to write them down. A good imagination is a wonderful thing. May yours always bring you happiness. Are Matthew and Marilla well? Can you give them my love? Do not forget to give Marilla a hug. Only do not squeeze her too hard. Not that she would not like it. Although she might pretend not to. Look out over the ocean. Do not forget the times we had there. School makes us forget friendship all too quickly. Can you promise to remember me? How can I ever forget you? Only one person is like you. Only one person is my bosom friend. Love always, I remain.

And then it is signed by "Belinda."

Holmes put down his tea, the papers and his pipe. "Could you please let me take a brief look at it?" he said as he reached across the table.

"If I ever seem to underestimate the ingenuity and imagination of an adolescent girl, Watson, you must say the word 'Avonlea' to me and restore me to reality. These two girls are truly quite remarkable are they not?"

"It would appear," I added, "that they had worked out their secret code together before they parted and are using it to convey revealing information to each other. Yes, very remarkable indeed."

Holmes read off the first letters of each sentence in the letter from Belinda.

"I A M I N H A L I F A X I A T T E N D S I R J O H N A M A C D O N A L D S C H O O L."

"It would appear," he continued, "that our time on this quaint little island will be all too short. We must be on our way to Halifax. Perhaps you could arrange a lecture visit there. Short notice should not be an issue as I do not expect that their fall social calendar is particularly crowded."

"I can look after that, Holmes, but your devoted fan, Anne, will be sad to see you go."

"Oh no, not at all. We must bring her with us. You and I must remain completely hidden from the enemy. Any hint that we are on to them would spell disaster. No, we shall have to take her with us."

"Honestly Holmes," I said firmly. "You cannot expect sober responsible people like the Cuthberts to allow a child to go travelling off in the company of two middle-aged men. Surely, that is impossible."

"As it is absolutely necessary, it cannot be impossible," he countered. "But as it is a family matter I will leave it in your good hands, my dear doctor, to convince the diligent guardians of the necessity. I will concentrate on the criminal matters that surround this case."

He rose and walked off the patio and back into the dining hall. Through the windows I could see him speaking to one of the waiters, instructing the lad to have his breakfast sent to his room no doubt, and then he departed so that he could have silence as he plotted out his next set of moves.

I sat for some time on the patio wondering how to convince two no-longer-young guardians of a unique red-haired girl to permit her to leave the safe surroundings of her home and travel with two strangers to the largest city in the region. I kept thinking about it through my breakfast and was still thinking as the hour of ten o'clock approached and I saw a familiar wagon and bouncing tresses of red hair ascending the driveway. I recognized the driver from the night before. The matronly woman who sat beside him, wearing a black hat and wrapped in a brown shawl, must be the dear Marilla, our newest Irregular's guardian.

I had the desk notify Holmes and I greeted the three of them. Holmes emerged and extended his hand to them in what I thought to be a more than necessary formal manner.

Sherlock Holmes ushered our three guests into the hotel's nicely appointed parlor. The shy gentleman, Mr. Matthew Cuthbert, looked very ill at ease and I gathered that he would far rather have been either in his own home or out in his fields than sitting sipping morning tea with two visitors from London.

"I do hope I haven't overstepped my boundaries, Mr. Holmes," began our young redhead. "I know that you only asked for me to come this morning but I knew that I would have to bring along Matthew and especially Marilla as this meeting had the potential to turn into much more than just a friendly chat about detective stories."

On this note Miss Marilla turned to Anne and with a look of perplexed indignation interrupted her. "Whatever are you talking about child? We are here to have a conversation with an important guest to our village and inform him of some of the interesting places and facts in order to make his visit more enjoyable. That is why we have come and for no other reason." She turned to Holmes and continued, "I do apologize, sir. Our girl, Anne, is a very good scholar and usually a real steady and reliable worker but she is afflicted with an imagination that takes her in flights of fancy beyond the realm of the practical and we have not been able, despite our prayers and diligent efforts, to cure her of it."

"Ah, but my dear lady," said Holmes. "A creative imagination is a splendid gift and there is, I must inform you, a far greater story behind our visit than any possible interest in giving lectures and eating lobster and potatoes, and Anne is part of that story. Is that not true Miss Shirley?"

Anne nodded apprehensively. Miss Marilla glared at her in incomprehension. I rose and walked over to Matthew. "Pardon me sir, but I need to chat with you about our travel arrangements. Would you mind stepping outside to the veranda? We can leave these storytellers to their imaginations." Matthew Cuthbert smiled and rose, relieved to get out of the parlor, and we found chairs on the porch and sat and chatted for the next twenty minutes. From time to time I could hear Marilla's voice gasping "Anne!" and I could only smile at what must be going on inside the parlor as Anne Shirley and Sherlock Holmes brought Marilla Cuthbert up to date on the evil doings of the Ku Klux Klan, all the things that had transpired over the course of the summer, and the role that her girl had played in bringing England's greatest detective halfway around the world.

Matthew and I returned to the parlor as Anne was finishing her narrative. Marilla was shaking her head enough to make it fall off. She looked at me as I seated myself and then at Holmes and exclaimed, "Doctor Watson and Mr. Holmes. What can I say? This is utterly humiliating. That my Anne should have imagined such a cockamamie story and sent it to you and caused you to travel all the way from London, well, what can I say? Honestly, sirs, we have tried our hardest to teach her to be honest and not give in to her wild imaginings. Please sir, accept our apologies. These things she has made up are absolutely impossible to believe. Completely featherbrained. I assure you that such a thing will never happen again..."

At this point Holmes interrupted her, somewhat forcefully. "My dear Miss Cuthbert. Permit me to assure you of something. While the things Anne has told you this morning are highly improbable they are not impossible. I have had her story confirmed by Scotland Yard, by the Foreign Office of the British Empire, and the American Department of Justice, and it has been brought to the attention of the King of England, his Gracious Majesty Edward the Seventh. It considered by all of those as well as by yours truly to be accurate and correct."

With the words "the King of England" Marilla's mouth dropped open and all words ceased. Anne's eyes went wide. Holmes continued, "The matters that she has discovered are not only true, they are of a most serious nature, and the threat to the lives and well-being of many citizens in several countries is being taken with the deepest possible concern.

"You have done well, Miss Anne, and on behalf of all those to whom I have referred, I thank you."

"Well then why, in heaven's name," Marilla exploded, "did you not say anything about this to me, Anne Shirley? You know that I will not tolerate your deceiving me. I am terribly disappointed with you."

"Oh please, Marilla," Anne implored. "I made a solemn vow not to tell you. I gave my word, and you know, as you have taught me, no one can go back on their word. If I had said anything it would have been a terrible burden to you. You know how Mrs. Rachel Lynde gets you to tell her everything, even all those things that you think are none of her concern. She would have coaxed the whole story out of you and then it would have been all over the island in a few days. And you have had to work terribly hard to continue to be charitable to her. And then Belinda would have been in great danger, and so would her family. Please don't be angry with me Marilla. I only did what I know you would have done had you been in my situation. You would not have broken a solemn vow would you? You wouldn't have risked letting Rachel Lynde know would you? Would you Marilla?"

Marilla said nothing and I sensed that similar scenes had been played out before between Anne and her devoted guardian. Holmes spoke and took control of the tense situation.

"My dear Miss Cuthbert, without Anne's help and her taking the initiative it is quite possible that terrible things could have happened. Those things are still possible and I will be depending on the unique role that Anne has established and her connection into the very heart of this evil Klan organization. We need her help."

"Hmm. Very well. If there is anything else she can tell you I suppose you should be free to ask. Go right ahead sir."

"Miss Cuthbert," Holmes continued, "our need is for much greater service than just asking her more questions. The information she has supplied us with has shown us that the activities of the Klan have moved from this Island and over to the city of Halifax. Dr. Watson and I must go there at once and it is essential that Miss Anne Shirley come with us."

This statement brought a snap of the head from Marilla.

"I beg your pardon, sir? Absolutely not! There is no way on earth that we would permit her to travel unaccompanied to Halifax with two men, even if you are a famous detective. That would be unthinkable. As her legal guardians we simply cannot permit that, can we Matthew?" She turned to her brother as she made uttered the final question.

"Of course not," said Matthew. "You are absolutely right Marilla. We could not permit her to travel unaccompanied in such a manner . . . to such a place . . . in such a situation."

"Well, I am glad you agree."

"Well then," added Matthew somewhat hesitantly. "if she cannot travel unaccompanied, then as her guardians we will just have to go with her and accompany her, won't we Marilla?"

"Fiddlesticks! Matthew Cuthbert! Do not be foolish. It would cost at least seventy-five dollars for us to travel to Halifax and back, what with the train and the steamer, and the accommodations. We simply do not have that kind of money. You know we don't. It does not grow on trees here in Prince Edward Island."

"Yes, Marilla," responded Matthew sounding defeated but then he tipped his head a little to the side and said, "No, money doesn't grow on trees here on the Island, at least not since we cut them all down for our shipbuilding industry, so much so that the industry died, gentlemen. So we will just have to ask you to cover our expenses, which I understand from the good doctor you are fully expecting to do, is that not right doctor?"

Before I could answer Marilla spoke again. "Matthew, there is the farm to run."

"Right you are as always, Marilla. Good thing I already have the harvest in from the field and the orchards. Martin, the hired man, can look after the cows while we're gone."

"Anne has her school work. She cannot possibly be missing days of school."

"Right you are Marilla. She'll have to bring her textbooks and exercise books with her. Mind you, you have always said that travel is the best education a young person can have. Much more valuable learning the real lessons of life than just book-learning."

For a moment Miss Marilla was at a loss, but she recovered. "Had it been at another time I might have considered it but I have an opportunity to engage in some piece work along with some other ladies in the sewing circle. We are considering an offer from a shop in the city and it could earn me at least five dollars a day. I am sorry but I am not in a position to turn down such an opportunity. So I will not be able to go and if I do not go then Anne cannot go. It is as simple as that."

"Well now, I dunno about that," said Matthew. "Five dollars a day is good money in these parts, and you're right Marilla, no sensible woman would turn down five dollars a day. Unless of course someone offered her ten dollars a day. Which is what I understand Mr. Holmes is willing to pay us. We would be his official assistants: you and me and Anne. That would be thirty dollars a day. And no sensible woman would give that up in exchange for five dollars a day."

Marilla paused and turned to Sherlock Holmes. "Sir you are very generous and yes that would be a very helpful amount for us to earn. Goodness knows we could use it. But while we are far from wealthy we are still proud Islanders and we do not take charity, not from you nor the government. There are folks who need charity much more than we do, and so you should be giving your money to them."

"I am not offering anybody charity," said Holmes sharply. "I am offering you short-term employment. The good St. Paul said that 'the laborer is worthy of his hire' and if I were not to give fair compensation for your work I would be acting in a most non-Christian manner, would I not, Miss Cuthbert? I am quite sure that you would not encourage me to do that, would you?"

"And you know, Marilla," added Matthew. "We could get you an appointment with the eye doctor in Halifax while we're there. Then you wouldn't have to wait another three months until he came back here. That might also be sensible, don't you think so?"

Miss Marilla Cuthbert said nothing as she glared in turn at Matthew, me, Holmes and finally Anne. Then she rose from her seat and looking down on the four of us announced, "Mr. Holmes, Dr. Watson, it will take some firm direction on my part but I am sure I can have these two ready to travel by tomorrow morning. As it is important that we be secretive about our actions then Matthew, Anne and I will travel to Belle River and take the steamer from Wood Islands and on to Pictou and there board the train to Halifax, and you, gentlemen, you will have to go back the way you came to Borden and Cape Tormentine and then take the train from there to Halifax. We can meet up at the Waverley Hotel. It is clean and safe and has reasonable rates and is close to the railway station. Matthew has made an excellent suggestion concerning my visit to the eye doctor. I shall book an appointment and then we will have a truthful reason to give to our friends concerning our travels as we would not wish to deceive them. Now we all have things to do so I suggest that we get moving."

With this she began to walk towards the door. Sherlock Holmes spoke before she had taken more than two steps.

"Excellent, madam. Excellent. However, there is one other issue that we must discuss and attend to."

"And what is that Mr. Holmes?" asked Miss Marilla.

"It will be necessary for Anne to re-establish direct personal contact with Belinda Openshaw. If Belinda's captors recognize Anne as the same young woman who befriended Belinda in Avonlea then it will arouse immediate suspicion and any chance for surprise will be lost. While Anne's appearance is without a doubt attractive and remarkable it is also memorable, indeed unforgettable. She would be spotted and recognized a mile away."

I felt so very badly for the girl. She visibly cringed as attention was drawn to her flaming red hair. She closed her eyes and winced in embarrassment.

"That should not be a problem, Mr. Holmes," responded Miss Marilla. "I am certain that in Halifax they have very fine salons for women wishing to have their hair dyed. Anne will go to one as soon as we arrive and have her hair color changed. Something close to raven's wing black should do the trick. It should wash out within a few weeks. As long as it does not turn green we will manage, won't we Anne?"

The young redhead said nothing. She just sat there with a look of shock and bewilderment on her face, then stood up and began to walk to the exit of the parlor, holding one of her long braids in her hand.

7 WELCOME TO AFRICVILLE

In obedience to the directions issued by Miss Marilla Cuthbert, Holmes and I departed from Avonlea at dawn the following day. By early afternoon we were in Halifax. Neither Holmes nor I had been in the city before. I racked my memory to come up with any details I might have read about it and could only recall that one of Sherlock Holmes's earlier clients, the lovely Miss Violet Hunter, had once worked for a Colonel Spence Munro who had departed England for Halifax, leaving her in the very peculiar situation recounted in my story of *The Adventure of the Copper Beeches*. Of course the entire world had heard about the Halifax harbor, one of the finest and best protected deep water ports in the world.

Once we were settled in the hotel Holmes suggested that hiring a cab to take us on a brief tour of the city would be a good use of our time. I heartily agreed and as there were still a few hours of daylight left and the weather was mild and sunny I quite looked forward to it. I had expected that we would take a tour up to the top of the Citadel Hill and enjoy an excellent view of the great harbor and ocean, or possibly a relaxed trot through Point Pleasant Park and breathe in the fresh sea air. But no, Holmes had other ideas mind.

"To Africville, please driver," instructed Holmes as we climbed into one of the hotel's livery carriages.

"I beg your pardon, sir," the driver replied. "But did you really mean to say that you want to go to Africville, eh?"

"Yes, my good man, that is precisely what I said and what I want," returned Holmes.

"Begging your pardon, sir, but it's not exactly the type of place that gentlemen like the two of you should want to go."

"And why not?"

"Well sir, please no offense eh, but it is a bit on the dodgy side and the two of you, well you just wouldn't fit in."

"And why not?"

"Well sir, no offense, but the two of you, well you just aren't the right colour to fit in your Africville. That's where most of Halifax's negroes live."

"And why should that be a concern?"

"Very well sir. I will take you there and drop you off. But please do not expect me to wait for you or come and get you after dark."

"And why not?"

"Well sir, I'm sorry sir, but I just cannot do that. It might not be safe, eh? You sir are free to take whatever risk you wish, but I happen to value my safety. So please don't be critical of me sir and please take my advice and mind yourself in Africville."

"Very well. We shall. How far it is it?"

"It's a fair bit sir. North end of the city. Past your Narrows, eh? At least three miles sir."

My hopes for a pleasant tour of the sights of the city had vanished and I was not looking forward to visiting a poorer part of it. But I had known Sherlock Holmes long enough to understand his compulsion to obtain as much data about all possible aspects of a potentially criminal situation. He had memorized nearly every street, alley, building, and shop in all of London, and I expected that he would be quickly adding the salient points of Halifax into his encyclopedic brain.

So we proceeded north on Barrington Street past the wharves and ferry docks of the busy harbor. Even on a Sunday boats were moving back and forth taking passengers and goods across to Dartmouth and up and down the channel. As we reached the north end of The Narrows I thought how very restricted the passageway had become and hoped that the captains of all of the boats would take care not to bump into each other. A collision could be a disaster.

At the limit of The Narrows the channel opened into an enormous inland bay, the Bedford Basin, and I understood why Halifax was renowned for its natural harbor. "Goodness Holmes. Look at this place. You could keep a hundred ocean-going ships here, maybe two hundred, and no enemy could touch them. One of the best naval harbors I can imagine."

"Quite so, Watson. I do not see any vessels here belonging to our Royal Navy, but perhaps someday they will make good use of the place."

A few minutes later the driver pulled his cab to a stop and turned to us and said, "Gentlemen, you're in Africville. Now please just mind what I told you, eh? Don't be hanging around here after dark."

I observed the cluster of houses that straddled a railway line. The village was obviously poorer that the other parts of the city but it hardly seemed dangerous. Most of the buildings were frame homes with clapboard siding, substantial in size, and colorfully painted. The roads were not paved but were clean and sided with ditches. Holmes and I strolled north along the main road from where we had been let off and, after passing the hundred or so houses of the neighborhood, turned around and walked back again. As it was a Sunday afternoon the children were not in school and there were scores of them playing various sorts of games in the road and the alleyway and in the central open space that abutted the houses.

"Really, Watson," commented Holmes. "Compared to the East End of London this village could almost be the Cotswolds. Poor it certainly is, but dangerous, ha, I think we would be more likely to be robbed in Piccadilly than here. These people all see seem to know each other and I am quite certain know everything there is to know about each other."

We stopped by the door of a substantial frame building, the Africville Baptist Church. As might be expected on a Sunday afternoon we could hear the loud but harmonious sounds of hymns being sung at the beginning of the Sunday School session. For several minutes we stood and listened as the words of *All Hail the Power of Jesus' Name*, and then *Hold the Fort* lustily sounded out from the open doorway.

"What say you Watson? Shall we venture in? I have no fear of either our being mugged or saved. But it would be a unique lesson in the social culture of this neighborhood." Without waiting for my reply he made his way to the door of the church. As we entered an elderly dark-skinned gentleman greeted us first with a look of surprise and then with a beaming smile, none the less radiant for the lack of a tooth or two.

"Welcome, gentlemen in the Savior's name. My name is Jesse Campbell, and whom do I have the honor of welcoming to our Sunday School?"

"My name is Holmes and this is my colleague, Watson."

"Yes, yes and welcome, and as do not stand much on formality here, sir, may I ask your Christian names as well."

"My colleague is John, Doctor John, and my name is Sherlock."

"Well, welcome Dr. John Watson and Mr. Sherlock Holmes." He stopped in mid-sentence and a look of shock came over his face followed by a mischievous smile.

"Now come on there, sir. You're pulling my leg. Your real name is not Sherlock Holmes is it? Your teasing an old man aren't you there fellow?"

"I assure you sir, my name is indeed Sherlock Holmes."

"But you cannot possibly be *the* Sherlock Holmes. The famous detective form London. Though I must say you do look a bit like him, at least by the sketches in the magazines. But I suppose you get mistaken for him all the time, what with the same name and all."

"No my good man, I assure you that I am in the flesh the Sherlock Holmes to which you refer."

"Well my goodness. My goodness gracious. Well now please gentlemen do have a seat in the pew on your left. I hope you will not object if I let our pastor know that we have a famous visitor in our midst." He motioned us to a nearby pew and made his way up the side aisle to the front of the church. As the entire congregation of upwards of two hundred people were on their feet singing hymns we remained standing as well and enjoyed the music, which if lacking in sophistication more than made up for it in enthusiasm.

A minute later another elderly gentleman dressed in a simple black suit and bearing a clerical collar came and stood beside Holmes. I could not follow their conversation over the music but after the hymn had ended and the people were seated Holmes turned to me and whispered, "We are being ordained as the preachers for the lesson. I trust you have a story at the ready, and I shall be giving the sermon. Be at peace, brother Watson, the new identity is only temporary and shall no doubt pass without any permanent deleterious effects."

The clergyman, who according to the leaflet in the pew was a Pastor Elijah Dixon, climbed to the pulpit after the end of the singing of the final hymn.

"Brothers and sisters," he announced in a rich baritone voice. "The Good Lord, who works in mysterious ways, has seen fit to bless our humble congregation this afternoon with a most unusual and unexpected treat." Here he paused and achieved the desired effect of the congregation's full attention. "How many of you have heard of the famous London detective, Mr. Sherlock Holmes? Let me see a show of hands."

Almost every hand in the hall went up.

"And how many of you have read one or more of the fascinating detective stories about Mr. Sherlock Holmes that were written by that wonderful writer, Dr. John Watson?"

Not quite as many hands were raised, but still the great majority of those present so indicated and I quietly chuckled to myself to see so many curious glances exchanged among the devout.

"Brother and sisters," Pastor Dixon continued, "as I said, the Lord works in mysterious way his wonders to perform and He has done that this afternoon. He has, in His wisdom, brought two very special visitors into our midst. Here, in our Sunday School, in the

Africville Baptist Church, in our very midst are Mr. Sherlock Holmes and Dr. Watson. In the flesh. In our midst. Gentlemen," he said, raising his eyes and looking at the two of us sitting in the back pew of the hall. "Could you please stand and let all of our people see that I am not joshing them and that we really have been visited with at least a minor miracle."

We stood and looked out over a sea of turned heads and dark faces with friendly bright smiles. Several of those sitting near to us nodded and said "Welcome" and other such friendly words of greeting.

"Now brothers and sisters, you remember from the story of Abraham how when strangers came before his tent he generously looked after them, and how the good St. Paul, or at least we believe it was St. Paul who wrote the *Epistle to the Hebrews*, reminded the believers to be hospitable to strangers for in doing so they might be entertaining angels unawares. Now I am very sure that neither Mr. Sherlock Holmes nor Dr. Watson would ever think of themselves as angels of light, would you gentlemen?" Here he spoke directly to the two of us and we vigorously shook our heads. We received in response a round of smiles and chuckles form the congregation.

"We have a choice to make, my dear people," resumed Pastor Dixon. "Now I do have a lesson prepared and am ready to deliver it to you, but I do not think the Lord would mind if we postponed that lesson by one week and called upon Mr. Holmes to give us a talk – perhaps the lecture he is planning to give later this week to the hoity toity of Halifax at the Strand Theatre – and then call on Doctor Watson for one of his stories. What do you say people? I don't think the Lord would mind all that much if we welcomed our visitors and you listened to them instead of me this afternoon. What do you say?"

There was a hearty round of "Amens" heard through the hall and a warm round of applause was given for Holmes and me as we made our way to the platform. For the second time in a few days

Sherlock Holmes gave a spell-binding lecture on *The Science of Deduction*. Given the sacred setting he omitted many of the salacious and titillating anecdotes with which he had warmed the blood of the audience in Avonlea, but he added some very recent data about the activities of the Ku Klux Klan in America, and particularly the crimes against negro people that had been committed by that evil society.

He also give an invitation for any member of the congregation, if they had heard rumors of any unsolved crime in Halifax, to write him an informing letter and send it care of the Waverley Hotel. When finished speaking he sat down but the congregation rose to its feet and gave him a thunderous round of applause. Holmes generally hated public attention but I could see that he was using this occasion to collect all sorts of data that might possibly be related to the situation that brought us to Halifax. Yet again I quietly marveled at the genius and imagination of his brilliant mind.

For my part I chose another one of my favorite stories that had been published in *The Strand* some years earlier and recited *The Mystery of the Yellow Face*. It began with a most perplexing mystery but concluded with a beautiful demonstration of the love that could and should exist between man and woman and children regardless of the color of one's skin. It was well-received and following my recitation I chatted with a number of friendly folks. I would never have suspected that my stories and the fame of Sherlock Holmes had spread even to this corner of the globe, but so they had.

"Back to the Waverley, Watson," said Holmes as we bid our good-byes to our congregation. I did not for a moment believe that we had enhanced their spiritual prospects, but perhaps their personal safety might be a little more in their minds in the days ahead. "By now our trio of Irregulars should have found their way there and we must diligently plan our next steps. We have our client's daughter still to return safely to her father."

8 THE MOUNTIES

We walked along the road parallel to the rail bed and out of Africville until we reached Barrington Street and hailed a cab back to the hotel. Our timing was fortunate and as we entered the lobby I saw our three newest recruits at the front desk. Holmes greeted Matthew and Marilla Cuthbert and Anne Shirley. They made their way to their rooms and would have carried their own bags had they not been intercepted by a couple of boys in hotel uniforms who relieved them of the exercise. Anne, in what I gathered was uncharacteristic silence, looked at everything around her in wide-eyed wonder. Matthew walked behind the assemblage, his head slightly bowed, holding his hat in both hands and looking as if he would rather be anyplace else on earth than where he found himself at present. Marilla played the sergeant-major and give directions to all within earshot.

At tea time we all gathered in the parlor and Sherlock Holmes laid out our plans, such as they were. The Royal Canadian Mounted Police had been contacted and would assist us. A member of their legendary force would be meeting us at the hotel after lunch. Anne and Marilla would make their way first thing Monday morning to a hair dressing salon where Anne's appearance would be altered beyond all recognition. Then on Monday afternoon we would travel in a closed carriage to Sir John A. MacDonald School where Anne would pick out Belinda and establish contact with her as she exited the doors of the building.

The twilight hour had arrived when our little rendezvous broke up and I took myself for a short walk - good for the constitution I always said - and strode as far as the top of the Citadel Hill, and enjoyed the splendid view of the ocean. As I returned I looked up to the roof of the hotel where they had built a small widow's walk. There was one lone figure standing there peering out over the harbor. The flash of red hair was unmistakable.

We went about our various assignments the following morning and shortly after the lunch hour re-grouped in the hotel parlor. Matthew entered first, followed by Marilla, with Anne in tow. I gasped at the change in Anne Shirley. "Oh my word, young lady," I expostulated. "You have become a raven-haired beauty."

The poor girl blushed, her flushed face made all the more apparent against the shining black hair. "Thank you, sir. I have dreamed my entire life of having black hair, or at least not having red hair. It is such a burden to be one of the few people on earth with hair so red. The one time I attempted to change my hair I was motivated only by vanity, which was a grievous fault, and the results were humiliating and disastrous and I swore that I would never do any such thing again. But this time I reasoned that I was not doing it from vanity, even if I do think the results are flattering, but my motives were pure and were only for the interest of my bosom friend who is in peril. Sadly the color will all wash out within a few weeks but while it is here I will exult in the change. And I do thank you, sir, for saying that it made me attractive. You have no idea how much it means to me that someone would say something so kind to me."

Marilla harrumphed. "Frankly with that pale skin of hers it makes her look like a ghost. Or more like some sort of ghoul, I would say. All I would have to do is paint some lipstick on her and she could pass for a vampire. Well, at least it didn't turn green, and the child is right, it is for a good cause."

A moment after we had all been seated a tall broad-shouldered man appeared in the doorway of the hotel parlor. He was wearing a bright scarlet tunic, black breeches, riding boots and topped with a tan-colored wide brimmed hat. At his hip was a revolved holster, attached to a gleaming black leather belt. A very impressive figure I must say, a member of the Royal Canadian Mounted Police, or the Mounties as they were known by all. What caught my attention even more forcibly was the massive dog that stood just behind him to the right. It was an enormous Alaskan Malamute, but even larger than the pair I had seen once at a dog show in London.

Dog and master made their way towards us. "Mr. Sherlock Holmes?" the officer queried. "Doctor Watson? Mr. and Miss Cuthbert? And Miss Anne Shirley?" he asked looking at each of us respectively. "I am Sergeant Preston, RCMP." He pulled up a chair and joined our circle.

I could not help myself and spoke up. "And Sergeant, are you not going to introduce your assistant? Who is this magnificent animal you have brought with you?"

The officer smiled broadly. "Ah, of course. This old boy is my loyal assistant, King. Part Alsatian and part timber wolf. We met when I was stationed up in the Yukon during the gold rush days of '98. We had some adventures up there, didn't we King?" He tussled the dog's head as he spoke and King responded with a friendly bark. "When it came time to leave, well, we were stuck with each other, so along he came with me when I was transferred down to Halifax. Brought your mate too, didn't you King? Your girl, Queenie. And three years back darned if they didn't produce a litter and now we have another five like this fellow, all trained and, if you don't mind my saying so gentlemen, the most powerful and finest police dogs in the Empire. We would put them up against your bloodhounds of Scotland Yard any day, wouldn't we King?" Another tussle was followed by another friendly bark.

"I must assume that he is safe and friendly," I said.

"Most assuredly, sir. He is the friendliest fellow on earth, at least to his friends that is. Not so much to those that aren't, if you know what I mean. Isn't that right, King?" (Another tussle. Another bark.)

"Well then," said Holmes. "It is a good thing that we are friends. I believe, Sergeant, that you have been informed as to the reasons for our being here?"

"Yes, sir. Our office had several wires from Scotland Yard giving us some information about the case. And then we had a wire from the Minister of Foreign Affairs in Ottawa telling us to give the case our undivided attention. You can imagine how that got things jumping over at our headquarters sir. So here I am, with King of course. [Tussle. Bark.] You have the services of every officer you need for this case, sir. It sounds like there are some very nasty things going on, or at least planned. And we want to keep the city safe for all of our citizens. So yes sir. You can count on us for this case, gentlemen, and ladies." He added the final note with a smile to Misses Anne and Marilla. Anne blushed and Marilla folded her arms and nodded back.

"How old are you, Miss Shirley?" the officer said abruptly turning to our red-headed Irregular. The girl was taken aback for a moment but quickly recovered her wits and answered. "Fifteen, sir. Actually fifteen and three-quarters. I will be sixteen in just a few more months, sir."

"Hmm. You should know, gentlemen, and lady," the officer replied, looking away from Anne and towards the rest of us. "That the RCMP does not normally allow the use of children in a dangerous police investigation. However, in this case it is obvious that Anne, and her friend Belinda, are the only contacts that we have with this Klan organization so we have agreed to make use of her, but I am under strict orders that I have to be close enough at all times to help should that be necessary. At all times."

"Oh sir," said Anne. "Does that mean that King will be with me too? I would feel very safe if I had you and King along. Especially if King were nearby protecting me." She rose from her chair and knelt in front of King, holding out her hand to the massive canine. "We are going to be partners, aren't, King?"

The dog looked up at his master, who gave a slight nod, and then King raised a large paw and extended it to Anne, who shook it, beaming a delighted smile while doing so.

"Anne Shirley, sit down," snapped Miss Marilla. "This is not the time to be playing with pets. Now get back in your chair and pay attention."

"Now ma'am," said the Sergeant, smiling at Marilla. "You might hurt King's feeling calling him a pet. He's a police dog and right proud of being so."

Miss Marilla folded her arms and nodded but said nothing.

The sergeant and Holmes reviewed our plans. At three o'clock we all met and climbed into a large closed carriage and made our way up and around to the far side of the Citadel Hill and parked about fifty yards past the doors of Sir John A. MacDonald School and waited for the school bell to ring.

"Are you quite ready, miss?" asked Sergeant Preston. "You know your job. Don't overdo it. Just make contact with Belinda and let her know she is safe. Follow her to wherever she is staying and let her know that you will see her again tomorrow. And then just keep on walking and we will be there to meet you on the north side of the Citadel Hill. Is that understood, miss?"

"And don't be flying off into any of your capers and imagining anything beyond what the policeman has told you, Anne," added Miss Marilla sharply. Anne nodded to the Mountie and smiled and patted the hand of Marilla. "I know you're worried for me, Marilla. But I couldn't be safer. I have King here watching out for me." With that she leaned over and placed a kiss on the top of the Alsatian's head. The dog gave a quick look at its master who gave a small nod and then King delivered one quick lick to Anne's cheek. She stifled a giggle, picked up her satchel of school books and made ready to leave the carriage.

The first round of children to leave the school were the younger ones and they let loose the universal screams of joy that are heard from school children in every land and nation around the earth as they are released from their confinement. They were followed a few minutes later by the scholars from the higher forms.

"There she is! That's Belinda. I'm sure it is." said Anne in quiet excitement as a young woman with hair even brighter red than Anne's used to be emerged from the school. "Shall I go now?" The Sergeant nodded and Anne exited the carriage and walked quickly to catch up with her friend.

Holmes, Marilla and Sergeant Preston all peered out of the carriage window. Matthew and I sat back as there was no room for more heads in the small window frame. We did not need to look however as Miss Marilla provided us with a running account.

"Belinda's walking along. Look, Anne's caught up with her," said Marilla. "Look at that, Belinda isn't even looking at her. She has no idea who it is. The disguise even fooled her bosom friend. Oh!

Now she knows. She's dropped her school books all over the pavement and is giving Anne a hug. Good gracious, Belinda, let her go. It's only been a month since you last saw her. They're standing chatting now. Oh. Now they're walking together down the road."

"Right they are ma'am," said the Sergeant. "We'll just follow them slowly at a bit of a distance. Anne won't go in the house, at least not today. We'll pick her up down and around the corner." He gave instructions to the driver and we pulled slowly away from the vantage point we had held. The carriage moved along at a distance of half a block behind the two girls. They stopped in front of a house that we concluded must be the one where Belinda was being held.

Marilla kept up her account. "Very well now Anne, just say good-bye like you were told. Don't be creating suspicions. That's my girl. Just give Belinda a hug and be on your way. Oh good. Belinda's turned and walked up the steps to the house. Anne is on her own now and walking down the hill."

With that Marilla moved back from the small window and sat back in her seat, her entire stout body visibly relaxing. The policeman and Holmes both had notebooks in hand and were marking down addresses. The Sergeant had a sketch pad on his knee and was doing a rapid penciled picture of the house and of the other houses, trees and roads around it. At the agreed upon meeting place we caught up with Anne and she climbed back into the carriage.

"Oh Mr. Holmes, Sergeant Preston, I don't know where to begin."

"Then don't," said Holmes sharply. "Do not say a thing until we get back to the hotel. Immediately, inside your mind, go over everything that you observed, everything that was said and make sure you remember them exactly as they happened. Leave nothing out."

"And add nothing," chimed in Marilla. Anne nodded, and said nothing.

9 I SPY

"Now Anne," said Holmes as we sat in the Waverley, waiting for the staff to bring a round of tea. "In logical order, tell us exactly what it was that you observed and were told."

"Yes, sir," the girl nodded. "I will do my best sir. "Really sir, it was all a bit jumbled, it was sir. First Belinda could not believe it was me and I had to explain all of why I was there and why I had black hair and not red hair, and I did not want her for a moment to think that I thought that red hair was not attractive seeing as she has red hair as well and is my bosom friend and she wanted to know then anything I knew about her father and I told her everything I knew from what you had told me and then she began to ask about Marilla and Matthew and Diana and Jane and all of the other girls in Avonlea and I tried sir, I really tried very hard to ask all the questions you had told me to ask but she just kept asking me questions but I tried my very best, honestly I did sir."

"Anne," gasped Miss Marilla. "Did you not hear what Mr. Holmes said? He said tell your story slowly and in logical order. Now stop running on so and just do what you were told."

CRAIG STEPHEN COPLAND

"I believe, madam," said Holmes to Miss Marilla. "It might be better if I were just to ask some specific questions. If that would be acceptable to you, Sergeant?"

"Go right ahead, sir," replied the policeman. "Otherwise we might be here for a very long time."

"Very well, then. Now Anne, is Belinda in any immediate danger?"

"Oh no sir. She says that they permit here to go to school but I would imagine that it is because she would drive them crazy, just as I would Marilla, if she were around the house all day so they send her to school but they warn her not to say anything to anybody or else her father will be killed, and she . . ."

"That's good, Anne," interrupted Holmes. "Who is living in the house with her?"

"Well sir there's the woman, the mean-spirited one I said had the gimlet face, that goes by the name of Aunt Morag, and she, that is Belinda, does not know if that is her real name or not but some of the other people in the house have called her by her last name and she, that is Belinda, says that her last name might be Murray, sir, and..."

"Very good, Anne. And are there others in the house?"

"Yes sir, there are two other men. One goes by the name of Horse but of course that is not his real name so I suppose it must be a nickname because he is on the tall and lanky side but his real name might be Harold, at least I imagine it might because she, Belinda that is, had heard her, Aunt Morag that is, call him Harry once or twice. He has an American accent which Belinda recognized as she has never lived in America after she was a child at the orphanage but her father grew up in Florida and has a similar accent but nearly as pronounced. . ."

92

"And are there any others?"

"Yes sir, there is another man, who is shorter and Belinda would not say that he is fat as that would be rude and being English and all she is not permitted to say rude things about other people even if they are true but he is certainly solidly built and he also has an accent just like Horse, I mean Harry, I mean Harold. And that's two of them along with Aunt Morag, that makes three, are the ones living in the house, and then . . ."

"Had she ever seen these men before?"

"Why yes sir. They are the ones who kidnapped her from her home in England. I'm sorry I forget to say that, didn't I?"

"Have there been visitors to the house?"

"Oh sir. I'm sorry. I know that was one of the questions you wanted me to ask but by the time we got through with her questions about her father, and about Avonlea, and mine about the people who were holding her captive, we were already at the house and she then wanted to come with me and escape and we had to talk about that, and she was very upset until I told her that if she just ran away right away then the police would not be able to arrest the men who were behind everything, and that her father would be in danger and so she had to go back into the house, and she was upset with my telling her that, and it took several minutes for her to get a hold of her wits so that she would not go back into the house looking sore distressed and arouse suspicions of Aunt Morag, or Miss Murray or whoever she is, sir. Oh, but she did tell me that she departed the house every morning at precisely 8:15 and I told her that I would be walking past her house at exactly that time and we could walk to school together but that I could not come into the school with her but would walk on past it. I hope I did not presume too much in telling her that but it seemed to me to be a good thing to do, and I hope that Sergeant Preston, and you Mr. Holmes, and of course King can arrange to deliver me to the place where you picked me up by 8:05 at the latest and then I will be able to be walking past her house at exactly 8:15 and come upon her as if by chance. I hope that is alright is it not sir?"

"It is totally alright, as you say," said Holmes. "I think we have all had enough excitement for the day and we should retire for supper and agree to meet in the morning at half past the hour of seven o'clock. And Miss Anne Shirley – you did very well today. I shall be honored to appoint you officially as a member of the Order of Baker Street Irregulars. Well done."

"Oh thank you sir. Thank you. That is a great honor sir; as great as I could ever aspire to. No one else in Avonlea, not even Gil … I mean not even any of the boys will have an honor like that. Thank you."

"And good night Anne," said Holmes with a warm and admiring smile.

"Such a shame," he said to me as we ascended the stairs to our rooms, "that she does not live in London. She would be quite the star among the Irregulars. Truly an exceptional imagination."

The following morning we assembled early at the door of the hotel. As we prepared to enter the carriage I noticed that Matthew had hung back and was not joining us. I gestured for him to enter but he leaned towards my ear and said, "I'll just stay here today. My old ticker is not too good at all this excitement," he said, patting his chest a little to the left side of his sternum. "There's a talk being given at the Agricultural College and I'll just take that in instead."

For the next three days our routine fell into place. Each morning we would depart early and Anne would meet Belinda as she emerged from her house of captivity and walk with her to the school, asking her questions that had been supplied to her by Sherlock Holmes and Sergeant Preston. They, along with Marilla and I and the massive canine, would wait in the carriage and follow at a circumspect distance. During the day Marilla visited the eye doctor and then would stand over Anne while she read her school texts and did her exercises. Matthew disappeared to find some fellow farmers that might have wandered into the provincial capital. The stalwart sergeant would return to his RCMP headquarters and Holmes would read the numerous letters he had received from the members of the Africville Baptist Church. Then he would head off to who knows where, but reappeared in time to join the afternoon excursion back to the school. I rented a day room on the top floor of the hotel and while enjoying the glorious view caught up on writing some of the stories about Sherlock Holmes's recent adventures.

On the Thursday morning Belinda handed Anne several sheets of paper which Anne in turn handed over to Sergeant Preston. The brave young lass had stayed awake for the past two evenings eavesdropping on meetings that were taking place in the parlor of the house between her captors and a few local men from Halifax. She dutifully copied down every name she heard and any other details of their conversation she could understand. Sergeant Preston looked over the papers and gave a low whistle of interest. "Well now, look who we have here. A few of these chaps are just our regular lowlife thugs but here's one of our bankers, and here's an importer fellow, and look at these two – they only arrived in Canada from Britain less than five years ago and now they think they should be the only true Canadians. Most of our negro families came here well over a century ago and these jokers have the gall to think that they have a right to be here and these dark-skinned folks don't. How do you explain that, Sherlock Holmes?"

Holmes said nothing for a moment and then turned to the sergeant. "Was it not Mark Twain who said 'Anger is an acid that can do more harm to the vessel in which it is stored than to anything on which it is poured.' These men, as with all of the criminal class, bring more harm to their own souls and to those they claim as friends and family than they will ever visit on others. As to why the souls of some men become angry and evil, sir, I have no explanation. Have you?"

"No sir. None," came the reply, with a sigh. "All I can do is assign some of my officers to investigate these fellows on the list. I can never hope to understand what would move them to harm their fellow man, especially these chaps who are by all rights quite well-off themselves. They want for nothing and yet they would take from those who have less. It makes no sense. No sense at all. Isn't that right, King?" (Tussle. Bark.)

On the Friday morning everything changed. The previous night the RCMP officers who had been watching the house reported that over twenty men had entered after dark and had remained until well past midnight. Most of them had been identified and corresponded to the names on the lists supplied by Belinda. Following their walk together on Friday morning we watched as Anne hustled much faster than usual back to the carriage. She hopped inside and I could see that her eyes were wide with fear.

"Belinda stayed up for hours," Anne said, sputtering to get her words out. "She heard them making plans and they were making terrible plans. They said they were going to teach a lesson to the city and remind everybody that Canada is a Christian country and that the only people who should be allowed to live here are those that are Protestant, English-speaking, and white. And they are going to do something horrible. On Saturday at midnight they are going to ride into Africville and burn it down. They will all be wearing disguises so no one will know who they really are. They will light houses on fire and they don't even care if there and mothers and children in them when they do. They are going to drive them all out of their homes and by the time they are done there will be nothing left of the village but a heap of ashes. That's what she said, sir. She was very upset, sir. But she wrote it all down and here it is Mr. Holmes, sir."

Several pieces of paper torn from a student's exercise book were given to Holmes. Anne stopped speaking and I could see tears forming in her eyes. Her face was flushed and her lovely young slender hands were trembling.

Marilla spoke first. "Anne Shirley, this is very serious. You are telling Mr. Holmes and a police officer that people in that house are planning to do terrible things; even murder. Are you very sure, young lady, that neither you nor Belinda is imagining any of this? If you are exaggerating in any way then there could be horrible consequences for all involved. Are you sure child?"

"Oh Marilla," said Anne grasping the hand of the older woman and squeezing it tightly. "I said the same thing to Belinda as you have said to me. We only had a few minutes to speak to each other as we walked to the school but she said that she would swear on the Bible that she heard them saying those things. She is so anxious, Marilla. She is in the depths of despair. She knows that if they are the type of people who would kill mothers and children that they would also kill her father, and even her. She begged me to let her come with me and get into this carriage and get away from them. I had to tell her to be brave and that she was being watched over but I am very frightened for her. Please Mr. Holmes. Please Sergeant Preston. Can we not take her away from here? Could I not just bring her to this carriage this afternoon after school is done?"

Holmes and the sergeant looked at each other and Holmes spoke first. "Anne, you and Belinda have been incredibly brave young women and if you are fearful for her life then by all means you may bring her to safety this afternoon. But I must tell you that if you do take that path it will be an unmistakable signal to these evil people that we are on to them. They will not be brought to justice and they will continue to be free to do terrible things to others in the months and years ahead. If their plan is to try to destroy Africville on Saturday night then there is only one more day for you and Belinda to continue to with your excellent work. If the two of you can do that it would be a great help to us."

Anne closed her eyes for a minute and did not speak. I imagined that she might be saying a prayer. "I believe, sir, that I could manage for one more day. I am sure that Belinda can do the same. She has been living in dreadful fear for months on end now. I am sure she could hold out for just a day more."

"Anne," said Holmes. "That would be very courageous of both you and Belinda. But it will not be enough if all we can do is catch these criminals in the act. We also have to be able to identify and track down all those who are part of their web. They are in contact with others of the same kind all over the world. They will have copies of letters and documents in the house and we have to be able to capture those as well before they have a chance to destroy them. Do you understand what I am saying?"

"Yes sir."

"Very well Anne. If these terrible people are planning to do something this Saturday night we no longer have the luxury of time. There is no school tomorrow and there will no opportunity to ask Belinda for additional data. But we must know where in the house they keep their records and correspondence. I so I must ask you to perform one final task and I will require your guardian's permission to do that." With this he gave a respectful nod towards Miss Marilla.

"What is it you want the child to do," said Miss Marilla.

"When you walk home this afternoon with Belinda have her invite you into the house for tea and then give us as full a report as possible of the layout of the house and see if you can tell where they keep all their papers."

"ABSOLUTELY NOT!" shouted Marilla in a voice loud enough to cause King to bark, perhaps in pain to his sensitive ears.

"Mr. Holmes, how dare you? You cannot possibly expect me to agree to let this child enter a home where you know there are people who are prepared to commit murder. I will not permit it. It is out of the question!"

Holmes nodded again respectfully towards Marilla. After a minute of awkward silence Anne spoke. "Did you not say before that Sergeant Preston had Mounties guarding the house? Several of them?"

"That's true, Anne," the officer replied.

"Anne Shirley" said Miss Marilla sternly. "I do not care if the entire British Expeditionary Force were guarding the house. You are not going inside."

"Sergeant Preston," continued Anne, giving the impression that she was well-practiced at being told by Marilla to stop speaking and doing exactly the opposite. "I have read that police dogs are trained to respond to commands given by whistles that only dogs can hear and humans can't. Can King do that?"

"He can. It is part of the training we give to all police dogs, miss."

"If I were somewhere in trouble but I had one of those whistles and I blew on it would King come to rescue me?"

"He would miss. Even if there were gunfire he would be there in seconds. That's what he does miss."

"Well then, I think I could go into that house if I knew that King were ready to help me if I needed it."

"Anne Shirley," snapped Miss Marilla again. "Dog or no dog the answer is no."

Anne turned her head directly towards Marilla and with a look that spoke of the presence of a young woman and no longer an innocent girl she said, "Marilla, I know that you care about me more than life itself and I am so very grateful for that. But my friend Belinda is in that house every day and every night and has no one at all to protect her. I just tremble when I think about her like that. If we cannot catch the entire web of these terrible people then she and her father will be in danger for the rest of their lives. I could not live the rest of my life knowing that I had the opportunity to change all that for her and failed to do it."

Here she paused and looked Marilla directly in the eye and spoke softly. "Marilla, Belinda is a frightened, lonely, heart-hungry girl just like I was when you first met me. You know perfectly well that if I were in that house and you were asked to do what I am being asked to do that you would do it without question. I know you would. And dear Marilla, you know you would too."

Marilla said nothing. Her face had lost all its color and her lower lip was trembling. The handkerchief that she had been holding on to was being twisted tightly and would not likely survive to see morning.

"Let me think about this. Let me think about this," she said while denting her chin with her forefinger.

The carriage had arrived back at the hotel and we descended from it. Marilla walked quickly into the hotel and emerged a few moments later with Matthew trailing behind. She made her way straightaway to one of the dog-cart cabs that was waiting in the driveway. We heard her give an order to the driver to take them to the High Street.

"We will meet back here at three o'clock," said Holmes. He took another cab and drove off. The sergeant got back into his carriage and left Anne and I standing in the driveway.

"I don't think I have ever been this frightened, sir," She said. "Not even when I thought I was going to drown and had to climb out onto the stump of the old bridge to keep from going under. There are people that I love and care about so deeply and they are depending on me and I do not want to fail them. Is that normal for people to feel that way, doctor?"

"Yes, my dear child," I said in my best doctor's voice. "It is entirely normal."

"Please doctor; do not call me a child. I wish I were a child right now, but I can't be. I have to be an adult and I do not feel at all ready to be one."

"Anne, you will do well. You are a brave young woman. You will risk you life to save your friend, and you will have King to come to your rescue within a few seconds. I have every confidence in you."

"Thank you doctor Watson. Thank you." She turned and went off to her room. I took myself for a long walk up the Citadel Hill and back again. A flood of long-forgotten feelings had swept over my heart. I knew those feelings. I had last felt them years ago in Afghanistan as my regiment prepared to go into battle. Although I was a medical officer and not an armed soldier I had come under fire many times and I knew there was a possibility of it happening not only to me but some my friends, old and new, before midnight the following day. It is a frightful feeling to have. It is also exhilarating like nothing else on earth.

After standing on the top of the Citadel for some time I returned back down the hill to the hotel. On the widow's walk on the roof of the hotel I could make out the sole figure of a slender young woman looking out over the ocean. The swaying locks of raven-black hair were unmistakable.

At 2:45 pm a cab returned bearing Matthew and Miss Marilla. She marched straight to the front desk and sent one of the boys scampering up the stairs to fetch Anne. A few minutes later Anne appeared, looking pale but determined. Her fists were clenched.

"Anne Shirley," ordered Marilla. "Come here into the parlor and sit down." Anne obeyed, looking puzzled. "Now," continued Marilla, "close your eyes and close your mouth and look up at me and do not say a word."

I resisted the temptation of noting that it was somewhat redundant to tell someone to close their mouth and not to say a word. I watched this little drama unfold in front of me and said nothing. Anne did as she was told and Marilla sat down immediately in front of her, not more than a few inches away. She reached into her handbag and extracted what I recognized as a tube of lipstick. She pulled off the cap and began to apply it lightly to Anne's lips. The second it touched her lips Anne opened her mouth and eyes and gasped, "Marilla!"

Her exclamation was met with a sharp rebuke. "I said shut your mouth and your eyes and keep quiet. This is necessary so that no one will suspect who you are, even those who have looking at you all summer. And if I ever catch you using this yourself before you are eighteen years of age so help me I will take a switch to your backside and send you to your room for a week. Now sit still."

Marilla finished applying bright red lipstick to Anne's lips, and then added a touch of rouge to her cheeks. The final touch was a ladies' make-up pencil that gave a dark outline to the edges of her blue eyes.

"Now turn around and let me get to your hair. Hurry up Anne, we haven't all day."

Anne turned her back to Miss Marilla and in less than two minutes her hair was twisted and pulled up behind her head and fixed with a series of hairpins. The change in her appearance was startling. The cheerful red-haired farm girl that we had met just a week ago in Avonlea had vanished. In her place was an ingénue fit for presentation at court.

"Well there. I must say," said Miss Marilla, "not a bad job in a hurry. What do you think, Matthew?"

Matthew was not looking at Anne but at Marilla. "Good heavens, Matthew, stop looking at me as if I just came from another planet. I was young once too and I do remember a few things that young women did to get themselves up and look presentable."

Matthew smiled at his sister. "I do remember Marilla. And a very beautiful young woman you were. I do remember. I remember very well."

"Well then stop remembering and give Anne that box you have under your arm. Anne, make haste and run up to your room and get into the dress and get back down here. Move Anne. On the double."

Anne took the box and ran up the stairs two at a time. While we waited for her to return Holmes and Sergeant Preston both appeared and looked impatient for us all to be on our way for our final data gathering mission.

"Sit down and let patience possess your souls," said Marilla firmly. "She'll be down in a minute."

Holmes continued to pace and looked at his watch several times. The sergeant scratched the ear of King until I was quite sure the poor beast was thoroughly annoyed by the attention. Out of the corner of my eye I saw a figure enter the top of the stairway and start to descend. It was a strikingly beautiful young woman in a black dress that came down as far as her calves. It had an empire waist the accentuated her lithe figure. Her shoes were shiny pumps with low heels and around her neck was a fine gold chain bearing a small mother-of-pearl locket. Miss Marilla and I caught each other's eye and she gave me a sly wink as it was obvious that neither Holmes nor Sergeant Preston realized that it was Anne Shirley who was approaching us.

"Please Miss Marilla," said Holmes impatiently. "Have the desk send for Anne. We must be on our way."

"Why don't you ask for her yourself," said Marilla with feigned haughtiness. "All you have to do is turn around."

Holmes did turn around and looked at the individual who was standing behind him. He broke into a spontaneous "Ha!" which is a close as Sherlock Holmes comes to laughing when in the hot pursuit of a case. "Oh my. Well done!" he exclaimed. "Well done, indeed. No one will ever guess that you were the same little girl that they saw running around Avonlea all summer."

Anne smiled sweetly at Holmes and nodded at the Mountie.

"It will be the boys in the senior form that we will have to be worried about," I offered. "Not the Klan."

"You won't have to worry about that," said Marilla. "Anne has been rudely spurning the finest young man in Avonlea for four years now. She will have no problem shooing off any would-be suitor."

Anne flashed a look bordering on anger at Marilla, who gave her a look right back. If words could have been attached to the look it would have said, "And you know I am right."

10 BEHIND ENEMY LINES

"Here's the whistle for King," said Sergeant Preston, handing a dog whistle across the seats of the carriage. "One short blast tells him to be on alert. Three means that there is an emergency and he has to come as fast as he can. We will be waiting in the driveway of the house on the block behind the you. If all goes well and you come out safe and sound, then just give one short toot. We will see King sit up and we will meet you at the usual place. If there is any problem at all give three hard blasts and he'll be there in less than five seconds, and he'll have three Mounties right behind him. You have that now, Anne?"

"Yes sir. One if I'm all right and three if there is trouble. I've got it, sir."

"And Anne," added Holmes, "we need information that is as exact as possible. You need to memorize every feature of the house. The layout of the rooms, the furniture, the lamps from the ceiling and on the walls, the bookshelves . . . everything. And it is very important that you try your very best to see where they are keeping all their records."

"Yes sir. But I am really not sure how to act sir. I do try my best at all time to be friendly and cheerful and I am afraid that if I start to speak that the awful woman who calls herself Aunt Morag will know who I am because that is the way I was all summer long and she heard me speak a thousand times, and then she will see through my disguise and it will be all over."

"Anne," said Miss Marilla severely. "I know that I have told you over and over again that it is a grievous fault to think uncharitably about others but on this one occasion only I suggest you try to act as if you are Josie Pye and not Anne Shirley."

"You mean give myself airs and act like an insufferable snob and even be rude to other people?"

"Yes that is precisely what I mean. And you have known Josie Pye and the rest of the Pye family for long enough to know exactly how any one of them might act and talk in such a situation."

A glimpse of a sly smile passed between Anne and Marilla. "I do believe," said Anne. "That I could act like Josie and keep it up for an hour. Yes. I could do that."

We reached our destination and Anne got out of the carriage. Holmes, Marilla and the sergeant arranged their heads in the window so that each could see. My curiosity got the better of me and I stood up inside the carriage. Standing on my tiptoes I could see over the three heads and watch the young woman walk towards the doorway of the school. I saw her meet up with Belinda, who stopped walking and stood and starred at Anne. The two resumed walking down the pavement away from the school and a trio of young men, all wearing their school blazers, dogged their footsteps. One by one each of them moved ahead and walked along beside Anne, and one by one they dropped back again a few minutes later, their drooping shoulders indicating defeat and a severe deflating of their masculine pride. I felt a profound sense of pity and sympathy for the young man in Avonlea who had been so treated for the past four years.

As the two girls approached Belinda's house of captivity both turned and walked up the steps and directly into the house. "She's in," said Holmes. "Now let us get to our station and be ready to respond if we have to."

The driver led the carriage around the block to the house whose backyard abutted the backyard of the house in which Anne was carrying out her mission of espionage. We pulled into the driveway and waited. A half an hour passed and we waited in silence. By the three-quarters of an hour mark I saw the sergeant looking at his watch. Holmes also leaned forward to glance out the window. Marilla was becoming noticeably agitated. Her handkerchief was in her hands and she was beginning to twist it. I could detect that her breathing was becoming quicker and shallower. The dear lady was becoming more and more upset with each passing minute. At the one hour mark I could see her body start to tremble and she fought to keep control of her fears. Curiously I was not the only one to notice. King, the massive canine, had been lying on the floor of the carriage resting his head on his outstretched paws. He rose and sat back on his haunches looking directly into the face of Miss Marilla and then he raised a giant paw and set it directly in her lap. She smiled at the old dog and said, "Oh you're getting worried too, aren't you old boy?" She reached out her hand and stroked the fur on the enormous head. King did not bark. He let out a low whimper and moved forward and laid his huge head directly in her lap. She stroked his fur gently but without ceasing.

Abruptly the dog sprang back. His ears twitched around. He turned his body and faced the open door of the carriage and slouched low as if ready to leap out to the ground.

"He's heard the one whistle blast," said the sergeant. "He's on the case. He's ready. He won't do anything unless he hears the whistle again."

We all held our breath for what seemed an eternity and then the massive dog dropped itself back to the floor of the carriage and laid its head again on its paws.

"All clear," said the Sergeant. "She's out of the house. Let's pick her up."

The carriage pulled out of the driveway and clattered down the hill. Anne was waiting for us at the bottom and jumped up into the carriage.

"I think I did it. I think I did it. They had no idea who I was at all. That Aunt Morag lady, she looked right at me and I gave her a snobby look right back and she just looked away. Oh Marilla, telling me act as if I were Josie Pye was the magical thing I needed. You really do have a wonderful imagination even if you keep on saying that you don't, and it worked."

"Excellent, Anne," said Holmes. "Now collect your wits and review in your mind everything you saw and heard. Don't say anything until we get back to the hotel and then tell us everything."

"Yes sir. Of course sir. But you should have seen how they re-acted to me. Belinda brought me in and said that my name was Rosalia, and that I had also just come to Halifax from England. I had been listening to her speak all summer so I could speak just like she did. It was her suggestion as we walked towards the house. She has such a wonderful imagination. Belinda introduced me and said that I had come from London, and Morag said something not very kind like, "Oh, not another one." And I just looked at her, because I am taller than her, and said, "Oh, and are you from one of those towns in South Carolina or are you from a farm?" I was truly very snobbish, and oh so very English all at the same time which is not terribly difficult because as Belinda says that they are one in the same thing.

"When the two American men, the one tall and thin and the other one fat, the ones that Belinda said had kidnapped her, came into the room I spoke to them as if they were the help and told them I needed some writing paper. Well, didn't they just look at me as if I were the Queen of Sheba, but one of them opened the closet under the central stairway and brought out a few sheets of paper, and I sat down at pretended to write out a poem for Belinda. But I could see where the paper had come from, and that is where they must be keeping all their papers and records and such."

"Anne," said Marilla, but in a gentle way. "I know you are excited and you did a very good job but now do as you were told and collect all your thoughts until we get to the hotel."

"Yes, Marilla. Only that I have to say that I did see, and Belinda told me too, where they are keeping all their papers."

"Yes Anne," said Marilla again. "Now take a deep breath and button your lip until we get back."

By this time we were pulling into the hotel entrance way and we all got out and made our way to the parlor where Matthew was patiently waiting for us. Holmes and Sergeant Preston sat Anne down and I could see them making sketches of the interior of the house. After an hour they rose and appeared to be ready for tea.

"Anne Shirley," said Marilla in a loud voice. "Do not go into the dining hall looking like that. Get up to your room and wash your face, and put your hair down and change your dress. The play-acting is over."

Anne looked crestfallen. "Oh Marilla, can I not just keep looking like this through dinner?"

"No Anne. You do not look at all like a good Christian girl from Avonlea should look, and that is who you are and you must remember that. Now get up to your room."

Anne was obviously not prepared to give up all that easily. "Marilla, I do not want to be proud in any way and I am not being boastful, but being as fair as I can be, I do have to say that I believe I have earned it this afternoon. So I think you should be fair."

"Oh very well then. I shall be heartily glad when all this fuss is over and you, well, you shall not be permitted to look like that again until you are eighteen years of age."

Tea and then dinner were pleasant affairs until Anne demanded to know what was going to happen tomorrow.

"My dear, Anne," said Holmes. "For you, I am afraid, nothing at all. Everything is now in the hands of the police and we shall all have to wait and let them do their job."

"Is there nothing else I can do to try to save Belinda?"

"No my dear. Nothing will happen until midnight tomorrow night. If the data Belinda has given us is correct then we will be prepared to round up the entire sorry group of these would-be Klansmen."

Having served in the Afghan War I knew from hard experience that there are many days when soldiers in a conflict just sit and do nothing. On some of those days you know that another regiment may be engaged in battle while yours waits around the camp. That is just the way these things happen. So I was willing to accept that our role had ended and we had to leave the rest of the battle to others.

Not so for my fifteen year-old fellow fighter. Anne was obviously distressed with the news that she could do nothing more than she had done, even if she had carried out her assignments with considerable courage and effectiveness. I had a few glimpses of her on the following day. She took herself on a walk down to Point Pleasant Park where she talked things over with herself, no doubt, the only way she could be sure of an appreciative and sympathetic listener. Later she was back and sat in the parlor with a book in her lap trying to read, but it was clear that she was not at all content just sitting and waiting.

The Saturday afternoon passed, as did the supper hour, with no news. Neither Holmes nor the Sergeant were anywhere to be seen and I knew that they were deep in preparation for the events that they expected to take place around midnight. At nine o'clock in the evening I retired to my room and once again picked up pen and paper and tried to think back to some earlier adventure and write it down. My heart was not in it and my mind was elsewhere. I could only guess how our young high-spirited redhead was fairing.

At ten o'clock there was a sharp pounding on my door. I jumped up to answer and opened the door to a young RCMP officer. "Doctor Watson? Corporal Renfrew, RCMP sir. Sorry to bother you doctor but could you please come with me at once. There is a carriage at the entrance, could you come immediately sir? And it's a bit nippy out there doctor. Best dress warmly. "

He did not wait for an answer but ran down the corridor and knocked on the room that Matthew was staying in. I dressed in a hurry and left the room. I ran into Matthew in the hallway, tucking his shirt tail into his trousers and pulling on his coat and hustling down the hall all at the same time. At the bottom of the stairs I could see Anne and Marilla standing in the lobby beside the young corporal.

"This way, please folks. Please we have no time to spare."

The four of us exited the hotel and I noted how the air had indeed become decidedly chilly. I could see the breath puffing out from the nostrils of a fine brace of black horses that were draped with blankets bearing the markings of the Royal Canadian Mounted Police. We hoped up into the carriage, followed by Corporal Renfrew, who shouted to the driver as he pulled the door closed behind us.

The carriage took off at a great speed and we charged through the empty streets of the city.

"I'm awfully sorry to do this to you folks," said the corporal. "I'm not sure exactly what is happening but I was sent to get you and told it was urgent. I believe it was because the Crown Prosecutor told my sergeant that it would be very important to this case if the same person who saw the people who are holding the girl at the house up beyond the Citadel could also be there to identify them if they showed up at whatever event is going to be happening tonight. Something like that. Sorry I do not know more. Wish I did. But I got my orders and they were as urgent as I've ever been given."

"And can you tell us where we are going, Corporal," I asked.

"Africville," he answered.

We were tearing up Barrington Street past the wharves and warehouses of the harbor and I recognized the looming mass of the sugar refinery that sat at the north end of the harbor. We rounded the corner to the left and ahead of us I saw the open expanse of the great Bedford Basin and then, a few minutes later, we were in the heart of Africville.

As it was now about 10:30 pm on a Saturday night I expected that the village would be alive with people visiting and enjoying each other's company but there was not a sound; it was like a ghost town. The carriage pulled to a stop at the door of the Africville Baptist

Church and the corporal bid us exit. "You're to wait here in the church folks. I'll be back in half an hour or so and maybe I'll know some more then. Please folks, inside the church. And not a sound. They cannot know that anyone is in there." With that he left and we entered the darkened church. The four of us sat in the same pew that Holmes and I had been in a week earlier, but the warmth and joy and friendliness had vanished. It was silent and chilly and more than a little unsettling.

Some forty-five minutes later the door of the church opened and the corporal returned. Behind him was an older gentleman that I recognized as Pastor Dixon. They approached us and the corporal said, "I need for you folks to make your way up to the balcony. There is window up there that looks out over the village. You can get a clear view of everything that's going to happen. But please, not a sound." Then he turned and went back out of the church and closed the door. The pastor locked the door and returned to us.

"Follow me, please my dear people. And don't worry. We're in good hands." In the darkened sanctuary we followed the old pastor up the stairs to the balcony and he led us to a window. With Anne's help he pulled up a few chairs until we had formed a small circle around it, giving the four of us a good view. The church was set off a little from the houses that sat in a cluster on the other side of the railway tracks and the dirt road that ran parallel to them. There was a thick copse of trees on one side of the houses, and in front of the cluster there was an open space of perhaps an acre that served, I remembered, as a play area for the children.

"Sir," I whispered to the pastor. "Can you tell us what is going to happen here? What are we supposed to be watching for?"

"I'm not entirely sure," he whispered back. "The corporal said that nothing is expected before midnight. That's all I know, sir. But you folks keep looking and I'll just keep praying and between us we'll be doing our jobs."

I smiled at the old man and noticed that his curiosity had clearly gotten the better of his orisons and after no more than two minutes on his knees he was glued to the window with the rest of us. Matthew stood up and moved away from the window and whispered, "The rest of you just tell me what happened. I don't think my old heart can watch without it wanting to stop and I'd just as soon keep it going for a year or two more."

Yet again we sat in silence.

"Do you see that glow at the far end of the road," whispered Pastor Dixon. "I'm thinking that may be our visitors. So bundle up folks. It might get a bit chilly over the next little while." He stood up and undid the latch on the window and lifted the lower sash until the space in front of us was wide open and we were looking out clearly into the dark village below us.

The glow was getting clearer now and it was moving quickly in our direction. Soon I could make out a small sea of torches bouncing along the road. Then I saw that there were some figures on horses and some riding in wagons. As they came even closer I could discern that the entire lot of them were dressed in flowing white robes, with white hoods covering their faces and white peaks rising from the tops of their hoods. When they were about a hundred yards up the road they suddenly began to let out loud shouts. Some must have had bugles and they began to blare. Others had cut off cow horns and were using them to blast loud squawks into the night air. The combination of their ghostly appearance, the thundering of the horses and the wagons and the cacophony of sound created a feeling of terror. I felt my hair stand on end. I could see Anne reach for the hand of Marilla and grasp on to it. Only the old pastor seemed to be quite relaxed, even enjoying the spectacle. What was truly strange was that there was not a sound and not even a lamp to be seen from the houses in front of us.

By now the horde of ghostly figures had reached the church and they moved around to the side of it where I could see them parking their wagons and tethering their horses. There were perhaps thirty in all, every one of them garbed in the same costume. Not a single face could be identified. They were all still shouting and blowing and making an unholy noise. They moved quickly, everyone carrying a blazing torch, and gathered in the open area in front of the first cluster of houses.

One of them moved to the front of the crowd and the rest of them fell quiet.

"Let this be a witness," he shouted at the top of his lungs. "Canada is for Canadians. Others are not welcome. Let them know boys."

He gesticulated with his torch towards the closest houses. About ten men ran past him and up to the houses. They smashed the nearest windows and tossed the torches inside and ran back to the crowd. I gasped. Anne stifled a cry. Marilla shuddered, "Those places are like tinder boxes. They'll be in flames before the families can get out. Oh dear God."

I could see that on the far side of the broken windows the torches gave a brilliant light and I knew that within seconds the room and then the entire house would be in flames. Then the oddest thing happened. One by one the bright glow within the house vanished and every house was once again completely dark.

A whispered voice beside me muttered, "What in the name of heaven happened?" Miss Marilla was as dumbstruck as I was.

There was silence from the crowd of ghoulish white figures. Then the leader shouted again, "You'll have to get the torches farther inside. Hit them again."

Another ten robed figures rushed past him to the same houses. This time they pitched the blazing torches like javelins through the now unobstructed windows. Again there was an immediate brilliant glow from the inside of the houses, and then again in quick succession the glows vanished and darkness returned.

"Hit the side windows this time," came the command from the leader. A third volley of men with torches rushed forward leaving only a handful of torchbearers in the crowd. They ran to the side of the houses and smashed another set of windows and tossed their torches inside and ran back. One more time there was a temporary bright glow from the interiors and one more time the glow vanished. Then one by one I saw a glow start up again in the houses and a moment later the front doors opened and from each house appeared two RCMP officers. One was carrying a lit torch and holding a revolver. The other had a rifle at his shoulder and pointing straight into the crowd of ghouls.

"Mercy me!" I heard Marilla sputter.

"STOP IN THE NAME OF THE CROWN! Raise your hands!" came the command from one of the officers. Several of the Klansmen began to lift up their hands but one of them shouted "RUN! GET OUT OF HERE!" The entire crowd turned and began to run for their horses and wagons. They had a good start on the Mounties and it looked as if they might reach their horses before the officers on foot could catch up with them.

"They're getting away. Oh no," I heard Anne cry.

From within the copse of trees I heard a voice shout, "ON KING! ON YOU HUSKIES!"

Out of the thick woods there bounded not just one but seven enormous animals, part Alsatian hound and part timber wolf.

"Its King," shouted Anne. "And Queenie. And their pups. It's the police dogs. Go King! Get them King!" She was standing now leaning out the window and shouting. Marilla stood up and put one stout arm around the girl's waist and pulled her back and into her chair. But a moment later all of us had our heads out the window watching.

The dogs were leaping and bounding and closing the space between them and the running Klansmen. All were barking loudly.

If you have read my story, *The Hound of the Baskervilles*, you will know that the sight of a gigantic hound in the night can put such terror into the soul of a man that his heart stops and he dies in fright. What I was observing was not just one hound but seven of them, all looking like terrible massive timber wolves and all bounding toward the now panicked runners. A vision out of Hell if ever there was one. The hounds had formed a running line and had caught up with the fleeing crowd. Then the massive beasts circled around in front of them and in trained formation spread out, stopped and faced the crowd. The runners halted and looked at the row of snarling fangs and teeth. The hounds moved closer to the Klansmen and the robed figures all moved back in unison. Again the growling hounds moved closer and again the men moved back, closer and closer to the wall of the church below us. By now the Mounties had reached the church and were standing behind the hounds. They had the Klansmen pinned up against the wall of the building, rifles lifted. There was no escape.

"Ha! Will you look at that Anne," burbled Marilla. "They got them. They got the whole bloody lot of those bastards." Anne and Marilla looked at each other and Marilla quickly lifted her hand to cover her mouth. "Oops," I heard her mutter into her hand.

"Now every last one of you," one of the Mounties shouted. "Remove your hoods and stand still and put your hands in the air. You with the torches, drop them on the ground. Now!"

All except one of the torches was dropped. One sole figure kept his in his hand and kept his hood on. He turned and with a blasphemous oath ran to the closest window of the church, and smashed it with the torch. The closest hound was on him in two fast bounds, but not before he heaved the torch inside the building. The hound knocked him to the ground and sunk its teeth into his arm. I heard a scream of pain but I was already on my feet and staring in horror at the blazing torch inside the church. It had landed near a side table that was stacked with hymn books and they were already catching flame. Within minutes the frame building would be an inferno.

"The baptistery tank!" I heard the pastor shout as he rushed past me. "There are buckets in the janitor's closet. I'll get them. Open the tank! It's under the pulpit!"

Matthew, who had been closest to the stairs, jumped down them to the main floor. He ran to the platform and gave the pulpit and muscled push and toppled it onto the floor below the platform. He dropped to his knees. "Here! Doc! The handles. Here! Lift!"

Together will pulled first one, then a second and then a third portion of the floor boards up and away, exposing the baptistery tank. The pastor appeared bearing three buckets in each hand.

"Form a brigade!" I heard Marilla shout. Matthew dropped to his knees and began to scoop buckets of water from the tank. He handed them off to me and I ran them over to the pastor who ran them to Marilla. In her lifetime she had hoisted several thousand pails of milk and she grabbed each bucket of water and tossed it directly into the spreading flames. Two buckets at a time she handed them to Anne who ran them down the aisle up the platform and handed them back to Matthew. The flames were moving along the wainscoting and getting stronger. Marilla was as close to them as she could bear and was being forced back from the heat. I heard pounding at the church door and in a moment of horror remembered how the pastor had locked it. The pounding ceased and the door crashed open. A rush of negro men, all bearing a bucket of water in each hand rushed in and up to the flames. Several Mounties followed them. One by one they tossed until the flames were beaten back. They joined the brigade and doubled up on the positions and ran the buckets back to the baptistery. Two of them were quickly down on their knees helping Matthew and one of them jumped right into the tank and began handing up buckets full of water to the waiting hands.

It was only some ten minutes from the time the fire started until the last of the flames was extinguished. The old pastor climbed up to the platform and reached his hand out to Matthew, helping to lift him to his feet and down the stairs. Then the two of them collapsed together on to the front pew of the sanctuary. Matthew had his hand on his chest. I walked over and sat myself, exhausted down beside them.

Pastor Dixon extended his hand to me and we shook firmly. In a loud rich baritone voice he said, for all to hear, "Will all the Lord's people now take note. God is clearly on the side of the Baptists."

"Pardon me, Pastor?"

"If we were Anglicans and all we had was a tiny font at the back of the church we have been goners. So Praise the Lord! I said Praise the Lord!"

The men from his congregation all enthusiastically shouted "Praise the Lord" in return. I distinctly heard Marilla's voice mingled with them, which was a small miracle in itself as she was a Methodist and not given to ecstatic utterances.

11 WHAT HAPPENED UP THERE?

It was two o'clock in the morning by the time we returned to the hotel. The night staff had received word about the events of the evening and had prepared several warm pots of tea and hot chocolate. We huddled in the parlor, miserably disheveled and exhausted but very wide awake. Not long after we were seated Sherlock Holmes appeared and joined us.

"Very well Holmes," I said firmly to my friend. "Would you mind telling us just what it was that happened up there in Africville?"

"Most certainly my dear Watson and my dearest and newest members of the Order of Baker Street Irregulars." He pulled up a chair and sat down beside us and reached for a cup of tea. Before he could begin his story I heard a cry of joy from Anne. I turned around and saw in the doorway the tall figure of Sergeant Preston, accompanied by King, and holding the hand of a beautiful young red haired woman. Anne leapt from her chair shouting "Cordelia!" and ran towards her and they threw their arms around each other. The Sergeant and the young woman joined us. Cordelia, or better known to the rest of us as Belinda, was introduced to Holmes and me. She gave warm hugs to Marilla and Matthew and sat down. She was wan and tired there were tears flowing from her pretty eyes but she was beaming with a smile.

The Sergeant looked over to Holmes and said, "I think we interrupted your story sir. Please keep going."

"Ah yes. And most important things first. At the very same time as the adventure was taking place in Africville several closely coordinated events were also happening. The house in which Miss Belinda had been captive was entered; all records were seized before they could be destroyed. Morag Murray was under arrest and Belinda was found safe and sound. Over in England Scotland Yard was carrying out a pre-dawn arrest of the network of Klan agents. A telegram has been sent off to your father, Miss Belinda letting him know that you are safe and in well and in good hands. I have just received his reply moments ago." He handed a telegram to Belinda who read it to herself and then dropped her head into her hands and sobbed quietly. Holmes nodded to the young woman and smiled and continued.

"We have also had word back from Washington DC. An officer reporting to President Roosevelt has cabled us to say that in several of the states they were able to use the records provided by Mr. Openshaw to dismantle much of the Klan's organization. Florida was one of them and those enemies of the Openshaw family are now behind bars. Unfortunately not all of the police in America are dedicated to the destruction of the Klan and it is still alive in many parts of the South. It may be years before it is destroyed, but we have certainly dealt it a serious blow and many terrible deeds that would have happened under their aegis now will not take place."

"Come on Holmes," I interrupted. "We can talk about Alabama later. What took place tonight? We were almost burned to a crisp."

"Ah yes. From the city maps and my analysis of the layout of the roads and houses it was obvious that if the Klan were to attack Africville it would have to be from the north, where there are no residents and only the abattoir, close to which there are no houses. The only logical place to gather to mount an attack was the open area across the tracks from the church. So with the help of Pastor Dixon every home facing that open area was contacted. All of the furniture was removed from the rooms nearest the windows and all were equipped with numerous buckets of water, several firemen, and two members of the RCMP. Three of the City's fire wagons, all loaded up with water and a team of firemen, were hidden in the block behind the open area. No sooner had a torch been tossed in through a window than a bucket of water was poured out on top of it and it was extinguished."

"That's all very clever, Mr. Holmes," said Marilla with undisguised mounting anger. "But why in heaven's name would you permit the attack to go ahead at all? People could have died. Houses could have burned down. Really Mr. Holmes."

"Miss Cuthbert, you are entirely correct. The problem we faced is that while it may be vile and stupid and disgusting to dress up like a ghost and say all sorts of horrible things about people of different skin color or different faiths, it is not against the law. Had we stopped the Klan's action before it began they would have all walked away scot-free. So this afternoon Pastor Dixon called together a special meeting of the villagers and we told them what we knew of the planned attack and gave them the choice. They could let it go ahead and we could put the Klansmen in jail for a long time, or we could stop it and leave them free to do harm in the future. The RCMP offered to cover the cost of any damage to their houses and the people agreed that putting up with some broken windows and wet floors was a small price to pay for the defeat of evil and the freedom to live in peace. So the attack was allowed to proceed.

Marilla folded her arms and harrumphed.

"We assumed that they might try to run back to their horses and wagons and therefore the canine unit was put into action. I believe that it is the first time the entire unit has acted together is it not Sergeant?"

"It was indeed, sir. First case they had as a complete team, and I must say I am more than a bit proud of them."

"As indeed you should be," said Holmes. "I did not see any Klansman drop dead of fright, although they had good reason too. Would you not agree, Doctor Watson?"

"No, none dropped dead," I responded. "But as a medical man I think I can safely say that several of them might have developed unfortunate urinary disorders on the spot."

Everyone laughed at that comment of mine, including Marilla, who let out a loud whooping laugh, and then covered her mouth her hand but could not conceal her wide smile.

"And the legal consequences for the perpetrators? What of that Sergeant?"

"Aunt Morag and the two Americans who took Belinda will be facing several charges related to assault, kidnapping and forcible confinement. They'll be behind bars for a long time. Every one of those blokes who tossed a torch will be charged with arson and attempted murder, and we think we can make those charges stick, so they'll be locked away for a long stretch as well. And as for those fools who have more money than they need and are still hateful and greedy, well several lawyers will help the villagers take them to civil court and sue them into bankruptcy. They will be very sorry. It will be a very big case here in Halifax. One of the biggest cases we have ever had to joy of handing over to the Crown Prosecutors. In one fell swoop a lot of bad men will face justice."

"A case for the record books indeed," said Holmes. "Doctor Watson, Miss Belinda and I will depart tomorrow and begin our journey back to England. Within a week she will be reunited with her father. I have no doubt that someday, Miss Anne Shirley, we will see you there. Bosom friends cannot be parted forever. Until that time this case shall remain one of the most challenging of my career. And you Sergeant? Where to now for you sir?"

"I've just had word that I'm being sent to Quebec to join in the hunt for some fugitive named Jack Flowers. That's my next case. But as for this one, I can say the same to you as I did a hour ago to my big old partner here."

"And what did you say to your faithful police dog?" queried Holmes.

"I said, 'Well King, this case is closed.'"

(Tussle. Bark.)

Appendix 1
Historical Notes

The events of *The Mystery of the Five Oranges* are set in 1908, the year of publication of *Anne of Green Gables,* by Lucy Maud Montgomery. The various events noted in Dr. Watson's opening reflection all took place in or around that year, as did most of the other events referred to in the story.

The steamship *RMS Lusitania* was launched by Cunard in 1906 and was the fastest way to get from America to England at that time. It continued to be a very popular means of crossing until it was sunk by a German U-boat in 1915. That act, causing the deaths of over 1,000 civilians, including 128 Americans, was one of the causes of the entry of the US into World War I. As a child I somehow became the owner of a few bubble gum cards that depicted historic disasters. The sinking of the *Lusitania* was one of them.

Prince Edward Island, with a population of only 120,000, built its own railway in the 1870s and the cost of building it led the island into bankruptcy and thus to its joining the other Canadian provinces and becoming part of Canada.

St. Andrews By-the-Sea is a beautiful small town nestled between the hills of New Brunswick and the Atlantic Ocean. The Algonquin Hotel with its magnificent golf course is still in operation and is a marvelous place to celebrate any worthwhile event or vacation. We chose it as the location of my 60th birthday.

The places referred to on PEI either are really there or are borrowed from Lucy Maud Montgomery. In the summer of 1987 I took my three daughters to see the Green Gables museum house. In what was designated as Anne's bedroom there was a school writing slate on the bedside table, broken into several pieces. I ignorantly remarked that it was too bad that someone had damaged the museum artifact, whereupon three adolescent girls, in unison said, "She broke it over Gilbert's head."

The Ku Klux Klan was originally formed by veterans of the Confederate Army following the civil war but it entered a dormant period shortly after that and did not emerge as the racist organization with its white robes, hoods and burning crosses until the years after World War I. It was active throughout New England at that time and spread into parts of Canada, and was particularly active in Saskatchewan. There is no reference to its ever having a local chapter in Nova Scotia and no raid ever took place in Halifax.

The references to the immigration of African-Americans, called "negroes" in this book only because that is how they were known in the original canon of Sherlock Holmes stories, are accurate. Thousands of them came to Atlantic Canada as part of the Loyalist influx following the American Revolution. Several thousand more came during and after the war of 1812–1814, and more arrived during the days of the Underground Railway. Most of the African-American slaves seeking their freedom however crossed into Canada at Detroit and settled in Southern Ontario.

Africville was a real community on the shores of the Bedford Basin in north-west Halifax where African-Canadians lived for over one hundred years. It was not destroyed by the Klan but rather by the governments of the City of Halifax and the Province of Nova Scotia as part of a well-intentioned but misguided slum clearance campaign in the late 1960s and to clear the way for the new bridge across the harbor. The place where the houses once stood is now a park and national historic site, and the Africville Church has been rebuilt and serves as a church and interpretive center.

Anyone who has read *Anne of Green Gables* and the other books in the *Anne* series knows that the places known as Avonlea, the Lake of Shining Waters, the White Sands Hotel, the railway station at Bright River and the house with the green gables knows that these locations truly exist and always will for they are real places in our imaginations.

Appendix 2
The Original Sherlock Holmes Story

THE FIVE ORANGE PIPS

ARTHUR CONAN DOYLE

CRAIG STEPHEN COPLAND

THE FIVE ORANGE PIPS

When I glance over my notes and records of the Sherlock Holmes cases between the years '82 and '90, I am faced by so many which present strange and interesting features that it is no easy matter to know which to choose and which to leave. Some, however, have already gained publicity through the papers, and others have not offered a field for those peculiar qualities which my friend possessed in so high a degree, and which it is the object of these papers to illustrate. Some, too, have baffled his analytical skill, and would be, as narratives, beginnings without an ending, while others have been but partially cleared up, and have their explanations founded rather upon conjecture and surmise than on that absolute logical proof which was so dear to him. There is, however, one of these last which was so remarkable in its details and so startling in its results that I am tempted to give some account of it in spite of the fact that there are points in connection with it which never have been, and probably never will be, entirely cleared up.

The year '87 furnished us with a long series of cases of greater or less interest, of which I retain the records. Among my headings under this one twelve months I find an account of the adventure of the Paradol Chamber, of the Amateur Mendicant Society, who held a luxurious club in the lower vault of a furniture warehouse, of the facts connected with the loss of the British bark Sophy Anderson, of the singular adventures of the Grice Patersons in the island of Uffa, and finally of the Camberwell poisoning case. In the latter, as may be remembered, Sherlock Holmes was able, by winding up the dead man's watch, to prove that it had been wound up two hours before, and that therefore the deceased had gone to bed within that time -- a deduction which was of the greatest importance in clearing up the case. All these I may sketch out at some future date, but none of them present such singular features as the strange train of circumstances which I have now taken up my pen to describe.

It was in the latter days of September, and the equinoctial gales had set in with exceptional violence. All day the wind had screamed and the rain had beaten against the windows, so that even here in the heart of great, hand-made London we were forced to raise our minds for the instant from the routine of life and to recognize the presence of those great elemental forces which shriek at mankind through the bars of his civilization, like untamed beasts in a cage. As evening drew in, the storm grew higher and louder, and the wind cried and sobbed like a child in the chimney. Sherlock Holmes sat moodily at one side of the fireplace cross-indexing his records of crime, while I at the other was deep in one of Clark Russell's fine sea-stories until the howl of the gale from without seemed to blend with the text, and the splash of the rain to lengthen out into the long swash of the sea waves. My wife was on a visit to her mother's, and for a few days I was a dweller once more in my old quarters at Baker Street.

"Why," said I, glancing up at my companion, "that was surely the bell. Who could come to-night? Some friend of yours, perhaps?"

"Except yourself I have none," he answered. "I do not encourage visitors."

"A client, then?"

"If so, it is a serious case. Nothing less would bring a man out on such a day and at such an hour. But I take it that it is more likely to be some crony of the landlady's."

Sherlock Holmes was wrong in his conjecture, however, for there came a step in the passage and a tapping at the door. He stretched out his long arm to turn the lamp away from himself and towards the vacant chair upon which a newcomer must sit.

"Come in!" said he.

The man who entered was young, some two-and-twenty at the outside, well-groomed and trimly clad, with something of refinement and delicacy in his bearing. The streaming umbrella which he held in his hand, and his long shining waterproof told of the fierce weather through which he had come. He looked about him anxiously in the glare of the lamp, and I could see that his face was pale and his eyes heavy, like those of a man who is weighed down with some great anxiety.

"I owe you an apology," he said, raising his golden pince-nez to his eyes. "I trust that I am not intruding. I fear that I have brought some traces of the storm and rain into your snug chamber."

"Give me your coat and umbrella," said Holmes. "They may rest here on the hook and will be dry presently. You have come up from the south-west, I see."

Yes, from Horsham."

"That clay and chalk mixture which I see upon your toe caps is quite distinctive."

"I have come for advice."

"That is easily got."

"And help."

"That is not always so easy."

"I have heard of you, Mr. Holmes. I heard from Major Prendergast how you saved him in the Tankerville Club scandal."

"Ah, of course. He was wrongfully accused of cheating at cards."

"He said that you could solve anything."

"He said too much."

"That you are never beaten."

"I have been beaten four times -- three times by men, and once by a woman."

"But what is that compared with the number of your successes?"

"It is true that I have been generally successful."

"Then you may be so with me."

"I beg that you will draw your chair up to the fire and favor me with some details as to your case."

"It is no ordinary one."

I am the final court of appeal."

"And yet I question, sir, whether, in all your experience, you have ever listened to a more mysterious and inexplicable chain of events than those which have happened in my own family."

"You fill me with interest," said Holmes. "Pray give us the essential facts from the commencement, and I can afterwards question you as to those details which seem to me to be most important."

The young man pulled his chair up and pushed his wet feet out towards the blaze.

"My name," said he, "is John Openshaw, but my own affairs have, as far as I can understand, little to do with this awful business. It is a hereditary matter; so in order to give you an idea of the facts, I must go back to the commencement of the affair.

"You must know that my grandfather had two sons -- my uncle Elias and my father Joseph. My father had a small factory at Coventry, which he enlarged at the time of the invention of bicycling. He was a patentee of the Openshaw unbreakable tire, and his business met with such success that he was able to sell it and to retire upon a handsome competence.

"My uncle Elias emigrated to America when he was a young man and became a planter in Florida, where he was reported to have done very well. At the time of the war he fought in Jackson's army, and afterwards under Hood, where he rose to be a colonel. When Lee laid down his arms my uncle returned to his plantation, where he remained for three or four years. About 1869 or 1870 he came back to Europe and took a small estate in Sussex, near Horsham. He had made a very considerable fortune in the States, and his reason for leaving them was his aversion to the negroes, and his dislike of the Republican policy in extending the franchise to them. He was a singular man, fierce and quick-tempered, very foul-mouthed when he was angry, and of a most retiring disposition. During all the years that he lived at Horsham, I doubt if ever he set foot in the town. He had a garden and two or three fields round his house, and there he would take his exercise, though very often for weeks on end he would never leave his room. He drank a great deal of brandy and smoked very heavily, but he would see no society and did not want any friends, not even his own brother.

"He didn't mind me; in fact, he took a fancy to me, for at the time when he saw me first I was a youngster of twelve or so. This would be in the year 1878, after he had been eight or nine years in England. He begged my father to let me live with him and he was very kind to me in his way. When he was sober he used to be fond of playing backgammon and draughts with me, and he would make me his representative both with the servants and with the tradespeople, so that by the time that I was sixteen I was quite master of the house. I kept all the keys and could go where I liked and do what I liked, so long as I did not disturb him in his privacy. There was one singular exception, however, for he had a single room, a lumber-room up among the attics, which was invariably locked, and which he would never permit either me or anyone else to enter. With a boy's curiosity I have peeped through the keyhole, but I was never able to see more than such a collection of old trunks and bundles as would be expected in such a room.

"One day -- it was in March, 1883 -- a letter with a foreign stamp lay upon the table in front of the colonel's plate. It was not a common thing for him to receive letters, for his bills were all paid in ready money, and he had no friends of any sort. 'From India!' said he as he took it up, 'Pondicherry postmark! What can this be?' Opening it hurriedly, out there jumped five little dried orange pips, which pattered down upon his plate. I began to laugh at this, but the laugh was struck from my lips at the sight of his face. His lip had fallen, his eyes were protruding, his skin the color of putty, and he glared at the envelope which he still held in his trembling hand, 'K. K. K.!' he shrieked, and then, 'My God, my God, my sins have overtaken me!'

"'What is it, uncle?' I cried.

"'Death,' said he, and rising from the table he retired to his room, leaving me palpitating with horror. I took up the envelope and saw scrawled in red ink upon the inner flap, just above the gum, the letter K three times repeated. There was nothing else save the five dried pips. What could be the reason of his overpowering terror? I left the breakfast-table, and as I ascended the stair I met him coming down with an old rusty key, which must have belonged to the attic, in one hand, and a small brass box, like a cashbox, in the other.

"'They may do what they like, but I'll checkmate them still,' said he with an oath. 'Tell Mary that I shall want a fire in my room to-day, and send down to Fordham, the Horsham lawyer.'

"I did as he ordered, and when the lawyer arrived I was asked to step up to the room. The fire was burning brightly, and in the grate there was a mass of black, fluffy ashes, as of burned paper, while the brass box stood open and empty beside it. As I glanced at the box I noticed, with a start, that upon the lid was printed the treble K which I had read in the morning upon the envelope.

"'I wish you, John,' said my uncle, 'to witness my will. I leave my estate, with all its advantages and all its disadvantages, to my brother, your father, whence it will, no doubt, descend to you. If you can enjoy it in peace, well and good! If you find you cannot, take my advice, my boy, and leave it to your deadliest enemy. I am sorry to give you such a two-edged thing, but I can't say what turn things are going to take. Kindly sign the paper where Mr. Fordham shows you.'

"I signed the paper as directed, and the lawyer took it away with him. The singular incident made, as you may think, the deepest impression upon me, and I pondered over it and turned it every way in my mind without being able to make anything of it. Yet I could not shake off the vague feeling of dread which it left behind, though the sensation grew less keen as the weeks passed and nothing happened to disturb the usual routine of our lives. I could see a change in my uncle, however. He drank more than ever, and he was less inclined for any sort of society. Most of his time he would spend in his room, with the door locked upon the inside, but sometimes he would emerge in a sort of drunken frenzy and would burst out of the house and tear about the garden with a revolver in his hand, screaming out that he was afraid of no man, and that he was not to be cooped up, like a sheep in a pen, by man or devil. When these hot fits were over however, he would rush tumultuously in at the door and lock and bar it behind him, like a man who can brazen it out no longer against the terror which lies at the roots of his soul. At such times I have seen his face, even on a cold day, glisten with moisture, as though it were new raised from a basin.

"Well, to come to an end of the matter, Mr. Holmes, and not to abuse your patience, there came a night when he made one of those drunken sallies from which he never came back. We found him, when we went to search for him, face downward in a little green-scummed pool, which lay at the foot of the garden. There was no sign of any violence, and the water was but two feet deep, so that the jury, having regard to his known eccentricity, brought in a verdict of 'suicide.' But I, who knew how he winced from the very thought of death, had much ado to persuade myself that he had gone out of his way to meet it. The matter passed, however, and my father entered into possession of the estate, and of some 14,000 pounds, which lay to his credit at the bank."

"One moment," Holmes interposed, "your statement is, I foresee, one of the most remarkable to which I have ever listened. Let me have the date of the reception by your uncle of the letter, and the date of his supposed suicide."

"The letter arrived on March 10, 1883. His death was seven weeks later, upon the night of May 2d."

"Thank you. Pray proceed."

"When my father took over the Horsham property, he, at my request, made a careful examination of the attic, which had been always locked up. We found the brass box there, although its contents had been destroyed. On the inside of the cover was a paper label, with the initials of K. K. K. repeated upon it, and 'Letters, memoranda, receipts, and a register' written beneath. These, we presume, indicated the nature of the papers which had been destroyed by Colonel Openshaw. For the rest, there was nothing of much importance in the attic save a great many scattered papers and note-books bearing upon my uncle's life in America. Some of them were of the war time and showed that he had done his duty well and had borne the repute of a brave soldier. Others were of a date during the reconstruction of the Southern states, and were mostly concerned with politics, for he had evidently taken a strong part in opposing the carpet-bag politicians who had been sent down from the North.

"Well, it was the beginning of '84 when my father came to live at Horsham, and all went as well as possible with us until the January of '85. On the fourth day after the new year I heard my father give a sharp cry of surprise as we sat together at the breakfast-table. There he was, sitting with a newly opened envelope in one hand and five dried orange pips in the outstretched palm of the other one. He had always laughed at what he called my cock-and-bull story about the colonel, but he looked very scared and puzzled now that the same thing had come upon himself.

"'Why, what on earth does this mean, John?' he stammered.

"My heart had turned to lead. 'It is K. K. K.,' said I.

"He looked inside the envelope. 'So it is,' he cried. 'Here are the very letters. But what is this written above them?'

"'Put the papers on the sundial,' I read, peeping over his shoulder.

"'What papers? What sundial?' he asked.

"'The sundial in the garden. There is no other,' said I; 'but the papers must be those that are destroyed.'

"'Pooh!' said he, gripping hard at his courage. 'We are in a civilized land here, and we can't have tomfoolery of this kind. Where does the thing come from?'

"'From Dundee,' I answered, glancing at the postmark.

"'Some preposterous practical joke,' said he. 'What have I to do with sundials and papers? I shall take no notice of such nonsense.'

"'I should certainly speak to the police,' I said.

"'And be laughed at for my pains. Nothing of the sort.'

"'Then let me do so?'

"'No, I forbid you. I won't have a fuss made about such nonsense.'

"It was in vain to argue with him, for he was a very obstinate man. I went about, however, with a heart which was full of forebodings.

"On the third day after the coming of the letter my father went from home to visit an old friend of his, Major Freebody, who is in command of one of the forts upon Portsdown Hill. I was glad that he should go, for it seemed to me that he was farther from danger when he was away from home. In that, however, I was in error. Upon the second day of his absence I received a telegram from the major, imploring me to come at once. My father had fallen over one of the deep chalk-pits which abound in the neighborhood, and was lying senseless, with a shattered skull. I hurried to him, but he passed away without having ever recovered his consciousness. He had, as it appears, been returning from Fareham in the twilight, and as the country was unknown to him, and the chalk-pit unfenced, the jury had no hesitation in bringing in a verdict of 'death from accidental causes.' Carefully as I examined every fact connected with his death, I was unable to find anything which could suggest the idea of murder. There were no signs of violence, no footmarks, no robbery, no record of strangers having been seen upon the roads. And yet I need not tell you that my mind was far from at ease, and that I was well-nigh certain that some foul plot had been woven round him.

"In this sinister way I came into my inheritance. You will ask me why I did not dispose of it? I answer, because I was well convinced that our troubles were in some way dependent upon an incident in my uncle's life, and that the danger would be as pressing in one house as in another.

"It was in January, '85, that my poor father met his end, and two years and eight months have elapsed since then. During that time I have lived happily at Horsham, and I had begun to hope that this curse had passed way from the family, and that it had ended with the last generation. I had begun to take comfort too soon, however; yesterday morning the blow fell in the very shape in which it had come upon my father."

The young man took from his waistcoat a crumpled envelope, and turning to the table he shook out upon it five little dried orange pips.

"This is the envelope," he continued. "The postmark is London -- eastern division. Within are the very words which were upon my father's last message: 'K. K. K.'; and then 'Put the papers on the sundial.'"

"What have you done?" asked Holmes.

"Nothing."

"Nothing?"

"To tell the truth" -- he sank his face into his thin, white hands --"I have felt helpless. I have felt like one of those poor rabbits when the snake is writhing towards it. I seem to be in the grasp of some resistless, inexorable evil, which no foresight and no precautions can guard against."

"Tut! tut!" cried Sherlock Holmes. "You must act, man, or you are lost. Nothing but energy can save you. This is no time for despair."

"I have seen the police."

"Ah!"

"But they listened to my story with a smile. I am convinced that the inspector has formed the opinion that the letters are all practical jokes, and that the deaths of my relations were really accidents, as the jury stated, and were not to be connected with the warnings."

Holmes shook his clenched hands in the air. "Incredible imbecility!" he cried.

"They have, however, allowed me a policeman, who may remain in the house with me."

"Has he come with you to-night?"

"No. His orders were to stay in the house."

Again Holmes raved in the air.

"Why did you come to me," he cried, "and, above all, why did you not come at once?"

"I did not know. It was only to-day that I spoke to Major Prendergast about my troubles and was advised by him to come to you."

"It is really two days since you had the letter. We should have acted before this. You have no further evidence, I suppose, than that which you have placed before us -- no suggestive detail which might help us?"

"There is one thing," said John Openshaw. He rummaged in his coat pocket, and, drawing out a piece of discolored, blue-tinted paper, he laid it out upon the table. "I have some remembrance," said he, "that on the day when my uncle burned the papers I observed that the small, unburned margins which lay amid the ashes were of this particular color. I found this single sheet upon the floor of his room, and I am inclined to think that it may be one of the papers which has, perhaps, fluttered out from among the others, and in that way has escaped destruction. Beyond the mention of pips, I do not see that it helps us much. I think myself that it is a page from some private diary. The writing is undoubtedly my uncle's."

Holmes moved the lamp, and we both bent over the sheet of paper, which showed by its ragged edge that it had indeed been torn from a book. It was headed, "March, 1869," and beneath were the following enigmatical notices:

4th. Hudson came. Same old platform.

7th. Set the pips on McCauley, Paramore, and John Swain, of St. Augustine.

9th. McCauley cleared.

10th. John Swain cleared.12th. Visited Paramore.

All well.

"Thank you!" said Holmes, folding up the paper and returning it to our visitor. "And now you must on no account lose another instant. We cannot spare time even to discuss what you have told me. You must get home instantly and act."

"What shall I do?"

"There is but one thing to do. It must be done at once. You must put this piece of paper which you have shown us into the brass box which you have described. You must also put in a note to say that all the other papers were burned by your uncle, and that this is the only one which remains. You must assert that in such words as will carry conviction with them. Having done this, you must at once put the box out upon the sundial, as directed. Do you understand?"

"Entirely."

"Do not think of revenge, or anything of the sort, at present. I think that we may gain that by means of the law; but we have our web to weave, while theirs is already woven. The first consideration is to remove the pressing danger which threatens you. The second is to clear up the mystery and to punish the guilty parties."

"I thank you," said the young man, rising and pulling on his overcoat. "You have given me fresh life and hope. I shall certainly do as you advise."

"Do not lose an instant. And, above all, take care of yourself in the meanwhile, for I do not think that there can be a doubt that you are threatened by a very real and imminent danger. How do you go back?

"By train from Waterloo."

"It is not yet nine. The streets will be crowded, so I trust that you may be in safety. And yet you cannot guard yourself too closely."

"I am armed."

"That is well. To-morrow I shall set to work upon your case."

"I shall see you at Horsham, then?"

"No, your secret lies in London. It is there that I shall seek it."

"Then I shall call upon you in a day, or in two days, with news as to the box and the papers. I shall take your advice in every particular." He shook hands with us and took his leave. Outside the wind still screamed and the rain splashed and pattered against the windows. This strange, wild story seemed to have come to us from amid the mad elements -- blown in upon us like a sheet of sea-weed in a gale -- and now to have been reabsorbed by them once more.

Sherlock Holmes sat for some time in silence, with his head sunk forward and his eyes bent upon the red glow of the fire. Then he lit his pipe, and leaning back in his chair he watched the blue smoke-rings as they chased each other up to the ceiling.

"I think, Watson," he remarked at last, "that of all our cases we have had none more fantastic than this."

"Save, perhaps, the Sign of Four."

"Well, yes. Save, perhaps, that. And yet this John Openshaw seems to me to be walking amid even greater perils than did the Sholtos."

"But have you," I asked, "formed any definite conception as to what these perils are?"

"There can be no question as to their nature," he answered.

"Then what are they? Who is this K. K. K., and why does he pursue this unhappy family?"

Sherlock Holmes closed his eyes and placed his elbows upon the arms of his chair, with his finger-tips together. "The ideal reasoner," he remarked, "would, when he had once been shown a single fact in all its bearings, deduce from it not only all the chain of events which led up to it but also all the results which would follow from it. As Cuvier could correctly describe a whole animal by the contemplation of a single bone, so the observer who has thoroughly understood one link in a series of incidents should be able to accurately state all the other ones, both before and after. We have not yet grasped the results which the reason alone can attain to. Problems may be solved in the study which have baffled all those who have sought a solution by the aid of their senses. To carry the art, however, to its highest pitch, it is necessary that the reasoner should be able to utilize all the facts which have come to his knowledge; and this in itself implies, as you will readily see, a possession of all knowledge, which, even in these days of free education and encyclopedias, is a somewhat rare accomplishment. It is not so impossible, however, that a man should possess all knowledge which is likely to be useful to him in his work, and this I have endeavored in my case to do. If I remember rightly, you on one occasion, in the early days of our friendship, defined my limits in a very precise fashion."

"Yes," I answered, laughing. "It was a singular document. Philosophy, astronomy, and politics were marked at zero, I remember. Botany variable, geology profound as regards the mud-stains from any region within fifty miles of town, chemistry eccentric, anatomy unsystematic, sensational literature and crime records unique, violin-player, boxer, swordsman, lawyer, and self-poisoner by cocaine and tobacco. Those, I think, were the main points of my analysis."

Holmes grinned at the last item. "Well," he said, "I say now, as I said then, that a man should keep his little brain-attic stocked with all the furniture that he is likely to use, and the rest he can put away in the lumber-room of his library, where he can get it if he wants it. Now, for such a case as the one which has been submitted to us to-night, we need certainly to muster all our resources. Kindly hand me down the letter K of the American Encyclopedia which stands upon the shelf beside you. Thank you. Now let us consider the situation and see what may be deduced from it. In the first place, we may start with a strong presumption that Colonel Openshaw had some very strong reason for leaving America. Men at his time of life do not change all their habits and exchange willingly the charming climate of Florida for the lonely life of an English provincial town. His extreme love of solitude in England suggests the idea that he was in fear of someone or something, so we may assume as a working hypothesis that it was fear of someone or something which drove him from America. As to what it was he feared, we can only deduce that by considering the formidable letters which were received by himself and his successors. Did you remark the postmarks of those letters?"

"The first was from Pondicherry, the second from Dundee, and the third from London."

"From East London. What do you deduce from that?"

"They are all seaports. That the writer was on board of a ship."

"Excellent. We have already a clue. There can be no doubt that the probability -- the strong probability -- is that the writer was on board of a ship. And now let us consider another point. In the case of Pondicherry, seven weeks elapsed between the threat and its fulfillment, in Dundee it was only some three or four days. Does that suggest anything?"

"A greater distance to travel."

"But the letter had also a greater distance to come."

"Then I do not see the point."

"There is at least a presumption that the vessel in which the man or men are is a sailing-ship. It looks as if they always send their singular warning or token before them when starting upon their mission. You see how quickly the deed followed the sign when it came from Dundee. If they had come from Pondicherry in a steamer they would have arrived almost as soon as their letter. But, as a matter of fact, seven weeks elapsed. I think that those seven weeks represented the difference between the mail boat which brought the letter and the sailing vessel which brought the writer."

"It is possible."

"More than that. It is probable. And now you see the deadly urgency of this new case, and why I urged young Openshaw to caution. The blow has always fallen at the end of the time which it would take the senders to travel the distance. But this one comes from London, and therefore we cannot count upon delay."

"Good God!" I cried. "What can it mean, this relentless persecution?"

"The papers which Openshaw carried are obviously of vital importance to the person or persons in the sailing-ship. I think that it is quite clear that there must be more than one of them. A single man could not have carried out two deaths in such a way as to deceive a coroner's jury. There must have been several in it, and they must have been men of resource and determination. Their papers they mean to have, be the holder of them who it may. In this way you see K. K. K. ceases to be the initials of an individual and becomes the badge of a society."

"But of what society?"

"Have you never --" said Sherlock Holmes, bending forward and sinking his voice --"have you never heard of the Ku Klux Klan?"

"I never have."

Holmes turned over the leaves of the book upon his knee. "Here it is," said he presently:

"Ku Klux Klan. A name derived from the fanciful resemblance to the sound produced by cocking a rifle. This terrible secret society was formed by some ex-Confederate soldiers in the

Southern states after the Civil War, and it rapidly formed local branches in different parts of the country, notably in Tennessee, Louisiana, the Carolinas, Georgia, and Florida. Its power was used for political purposes, principally for the terrorizing of the negro voters and the murdering and driving from the country of those who were opposed to its views. Its outrages were usually preceded by a warning sent to the marked man in some fantastic but generally recognized shape -- a sprig of oak-leaves in some parts, melon seeds or orange pips in others. On receiving this the victim might either openly abjure his former ways, or might fly from the country. If he braved the matter out, death would unfailingly come upon him, and usually in some strange and unforeseen manner. So perfect was the organization of the society, and so systematic its methods, that there is hardly a case upon record where any man succeeded in braving it with impunity, or in which any of its outrages were traced home to the perpetrators. For some years the organization flourished in spite of the efforts of the United States government and of the better classes of the community in the South. Eventually, in the year 1869, the movement rather suddenly collapsed, although there have been sporadic outbreaks of the same sort since that date.

"You will observe," said Holmes, laying down the volume, "that the sudden breaking up of the society was coincident with the disappearance of Openshaw from America with their papers. It may well have been cause and effect. It is no wonder that he and his family have some of the more implacable spirits upon their track. You can understand that this register and diary may implicate some of the first men in the South, and that there may be many who will not sleep easy at night until it is recovered."

"Then the page we have seen --"

"Is such as we might expect. It ran, if I remember right, 'sent the pips to A, B, and C' -- that is, sent the society's warning to them. Then there are successive entries that A and B cleared, or left the country, and finally that C was visited, with, I fear, a sinister result for C. Well, I think, Doctor, that we may let some light into this dark place, and I believe that the only chance young Openshaw has in the meantime is to do what I have told him. There is nothing more to be said or to be done to-night, so hand me over my violin and let us try to forget for half an hour the miserable weather and the still more miserable ways of our fellow-men."

It had cleared in the morning, and the sun was shining with a subdued brightness through the dim veil which hangs over the great city. Sherlock Holmes was already at breakfast when I came down.

"You will excuse me for not waiting for you," said he; "I have, I foresee, a very busy day before me in looking into this case of young Openshaw's."

"What steps will you take?" I asked.

"It will very much depend upon the results of my first inquiries. I may have to go down to Horsham, after all."

"You will not go there first?"

"No, I shall commence with the City. Just ring the bell and the maid will bring up your coffee."

As I waited, I lifted the unopened newspaper from the table and glanced my eye over it. It rested upon a heading which sent a chill to my heart.

"Holmes," I cried, "you are too late."

"Ah!" said he, laying down his cup, "I feared as much. How was it done?" He spoke calmly, but I could see that he was deeply moved.

"My eye caught the name of Openshaw, and the heading 'Tragedy Near Waterloo Bridge.' Here is the account:

"Between nine and ten last night Police-Constable Cook, of the H Division, on duty near Waterloo Bridge, heard a cry for help and a splash in the water. The night, however, was extremely dark and stormy, so that, in spite of the help of several passers-by, it was quite impossible to effect a rescue. The alarm, however, was given, and, by the aid of the water-police, the body was eventually recovered. It proved to be that of a young gentleman whose name, as it appears from an envelope which was found in his pocket, was John Openshaw, and whose residence is near Horsham. It is conjectured that he may have been hurrying down to catch the last train from Waterloo Station, and that in his haste and the extreme darkness he missed his path and walked over the edge of one of the small landing-places for river steamboats. The body exhibited no traces of violence, and there can be no doubt that the deceased had been the victim of an unfortunate accident, which should have the effect of calling the attention of the authorities to the condition of the riverside landing-stages."

We sat in silence for some minutes, Holmes more depressed and shaken than I had ever seen him.

"That hurts my pride, Watson," he said at last. "It is a petty feeling, no doubt, but it hurts my pride. It becomes a personal matter with me now, and, if God sends me health, I shall set my hand upon this gang. That he should come to me for help, and that I should send him away to his death -- !" He sprang from his chair and paced about the room in uncontrollable agitation, with a flush upon his sallow cheeks and a nervous clasping and unclasping of his long thin hands.

"They must be cunning devils," he exclaimed at last. "How could they have decoyed him down there? The Embankment is not on the direct line to the station. The bridge, no doubt, was too crowded, even on such a night, for their purpose. Well, Watson, we shall see who will win in the long run. I am going out now!"

"To the police?"

"No; I shall be my own police. When I have spun the web they may take the flies, but not before."

All day I was engaged in my professional work, and it was late in the evening before I returned to Baker Street. Sherlock Holmes had not come back yet. It was nearly ten o'clock before he entered, looking pale and worn. He walked up to the sideboard, and tearing a piece from the loaf he devoured it voraciously, washing it down with a long draught of water.

"You are hungry," I remarked.

"Starving. It had escaped my memory. I have had nothing since breakfast."

"Nothing?"

"Not a bite. I had no time to think of it."

"And how have you succeeded?"

"Well."

"You have a clue?"

"I have them in the hollow of my hand. Young Openshaw shall not long remain unavenged. Why, Watson, let us put their own devilish trade-mark upon them. It is well thought of!"

"What do you mean?"

He took an orange from the cupboard, and tearing it to pieces he squeezed out the pips upon the table. Of these he took five and thrust them into an envelope. On the inside of the flap he wrote

THE FIVE PIPS

"S. H. for J. O." Then he sealed it and addressed it to "Captain James Calhoun, Bark Lone Star, Savannah, Georgia."

"That will await him when he enters port," said he, chuckling. "It may give him a sleepless night. He will find it as sure a precursor of his fate as Openshaw did before him."

"And who is this Captain Calhoun?"

"The leader of the gang. I shall have the others, but he first."

"How did you trace it, then?"

He took a large sheet of paper from his pocket, all covered with dates and names.

"I have spent the whole day," said he, "over Lloyd's registers and files of the old papers, following the future career of every vessel which touched at Pondicherry in January and February in '83. There were thirty-six ships of fair tonnage which were reported there during those months. Of these, one, the Lone Star, instantly attracted my attention, since, although it was reported as having cleared from London, the name is that which is given to one of the states of the Union."

"Texas, I think."

"I was not and am not sure which; but I knew that the ship must have an American origin."

"What then?"

"I searched the Dundee records, and when I found that the bark Lone Star was there in January, '85, my suspicion became a certainty. I then inquired as to the vessels which lay at present in the port of London."

"Yes?"

"The Lone Star had arrived here last week. I went down to the Albert Dock and found that she had been taken down the river by the early tide this morning, homeward bound to Savannah. I wired to Gravesend and learned that she had passed some time ago, and as the wind is easterly I have no doubt that she is now past the Goodwins and not very far from the Isle of Wight."

"What will you do, then?"

"Oh, I have my hand upon him. He and the two mates, are as I learn, the only native-born Americans in the ship. The others are Finns and Germans. I know, also, that they were all three away from the ship last night. I had it from the stevedore who has been loading their cargo. By the time that their sailing-ship reaches Savannah the mail-boat will have carried this letter, and the cable will have informed the police of Savannah that these three gentlemen are badly wanted here upon a charge of murder."

There is ever a flaw, however, in the best laid of human plans, and the murderers of John Openshaw were never to receive the orange pips which would show them that another, as cunning and as resolute as themselves, was upon their track. Very long and very severe were the equinoctial gales that year. We waited long for news of the Lone Star of Savannah, but none ever reached us. We did at last hear that somewhere far out in the Atlantic a shattered stern-post of the boat was seen swinging in the trough of a wave, with the letters "L. S." carved upon it, and that is all which we shall ever know of the fate of the Lone Star.

ABOUT THE AUTHOR

Once upon a time Craig Stephen Copland was an English major and studied under both Northrop Frye and Marshall McLuhan at the University of Toronto way back in the 1960's. He never got over his spiritual attraction to great literature and captivating stories. Somewhere in the decades since, he became a Sherlockian. He is a recent member of the Bootmakers of Toronto (www.torontobootmakers.com), and mildly addicted to the sacred canon. In real life he writes about and serves as a consultant for political campaigns in Canada and the USA (www.ConservativeGrowth.net), but would abandon that pursuit if he could possibly earn a decent living writing about Sherlock Holmes.

If you enjoyed this new Sherlock Holmes mystery please take a minute and write a review on Amazon and let others know about it.

Thank you.

CSC

Other New Sherlock Holmes Mysteries
by Craig Stephen Copland

Available from Amazon as either ebook or paperback.

Studying Scarlet. Starlet O'Halloran has arrived in London looking for her long lost husband Brett. She and Momma come to 221B Baker Street seeking the help of Sherlock Holmes. Unexpected events unfold and together Sherlock Holmes, Dr. Watson, Starlet, Brett, and two new members of the clan have to vanquish a band of murderous anarchists, rescue the King and save the British Empire. This is an unau thorized parody inspired by Arthur Conan Doyle's *A Study in Scarlett* and Margaret Mitchell's *Gone with the Wind.*

The Bald-Headed Trust. Watson insists on taking Sherlock Holmes on a short vacation to the seaside in Plymouth. No sooner has Holmes arrived than he is needed to solve a double murder and prevent a massive fraud diabolically designed by the evil Professor himself. Who knew that a family of devout conservative churchgoers could come to the aid of Sherlock Holmes and bring enormous grief to evil doers? The story is inspired by *The Red-Headed League*, one of the original stories in the canon of Sherlock Holmes by Sir Arthur Conan Doyle.

A Scandal in Fordlandia. Another parody- this one inspired by *A Scandal in Bohemia* and set in Toronto in 2014. Sherlock Holmes and Dr. Watson are visited by Toronto's famous (infamous?) mayor. When he was a teenager someone took some nasty photos of him and if they are made public, disaster could come not only upon those in the photo but on all of civilization as we know it. Holmes and Watson must retrieve the photos before they are printed in the unfriendly press.

The Hudson Valley Mystery. A young man in New York went mad and murdered his father. His mother knows he is innocent and knows he is not crazy. She appeals to Sherlock Holmes and together with Dr. and Mrs. Watson he crosses the Atlantic to help this client in need. Once there they must duel with the villains of Tammany hall and with the specter of the legendary headless horseman. Inspired by *The Buscombe Valley Mystery.*

A Case of Identity Theft. It is the fall of 1888 and Jack the Ripper is terrorizing London. A young married couple are found, minus their heads. Another young couple is missing and in peril. Sherlock Holmes, Dr. Watson, the couple's mothers, and Mycroft must join forces to find the murderer before he kills again and makes off with half a million pounds. The novella is inspired by *A Case of Identity* and the text of the original Sherlock Holmes story is included in the paperback version.

www.SherlockHolmesMystery.com

A NEW SHERLOCK HOLMES MYSTERY

THE SIGN
OF THE THIRD

CRAIG STEPHEN COPLAND

The Sign of the Third. Fifteen hundred years ago the courageous Princess Hemamali smuggled the sacred tooth of the Buddha into Ceylon. Since that time it has never left the Temple of the Tooth in Kandy, where it has been guarded and worshiped by the faithful. Now, for the first time, it is being brought to London to be part of a magnificent exhibit at the British Museum. But what if something were to happen to it? It would be a disaster for the British Empire. Sherlock Holmes, Dr. Watson and even Mycroft Holmes are called upon to prevent such a crisis. Will they prevail? What is about to happen to Dr. John Watson? And who is this mysterious young Irregular they call The Injin? This novella is inspired by the Sherlock Holmes mystery, *The Sign of the Four*. The same characters and villains are present, and fans of Arthur Conan Doyle's Sherlock Holmes will enjoy seeing their hero called upon yet again to use his powers of scientific deduction to thwart dangerous and dastardly criminals. The text of the original story, *The Sign of the Four*, is included in the paperback version. Your enjoyment of the book will be enhanced by re-reading the Sherlock Holmes classic and then seeing what new adventures are in store.

19439519R10099

Made in the USA
Middletown, DE
19 April 2015